Midnight
by

Kathi Daley

I want to thank the very talented Jessica Fischer for the cover art.

I so appreciate Bruce Curran, who is always ready and willing to answer my cyber questions, and Peggy Hyndman, for helping sleuth out those pesky typos.

A special thank you to Joanne Kocourek, Darla Taylor, Patty Liu, and Vivian Shane for submitting recipes.

And, of course, thanks to the readers and bloggers in my life, who make doing what I do possible.

Thank you to Randy Ladenheim-Gil for the editing.

And finally I want to thank my sister Christy for always lending an ear and my husband Ken for allowing me time to write by taking care of everything else.

Books by Kathi Daley

Come for the murder, stay for the romance.

Zoe Donovan Cozy Mystery:
Halloween Hijinks
The Trouble With Turkeys
Christmas Crazy
Cupid's Curse
Big Bunny Bump-off
Beach Blanket Barbie
Maui Madness
Derby Divas
Haunted Hamlet
Turkeys, Tuxes, and Tabbies
Christmas Cozy
Alaskan Alliance
Matrimony Meltdown
Soul Surrender
Heavenly Honeymoon
Hopscotch Homicide
Ghostly Graveyard
Santa Sleuth
Shamrock Shenanigans
Kitten Kaboodle
Costume Catastrophe
Candy Cane Caper
Holiday Hangover
Easter Escapade
Camp Carter
Trick or Treason
Reindeer Roundup – *December 2017*

Zimmerman Academy The New Normal

Ashton Falls Cozy Cookbook

Tj Jensen Paradise Lake Mysteries by Henery Press:

Pumpkins in Paradise
Snowmen in Paradise
Bikinis in Paradise
Christmas in Paradise
Puppies in Paradise
Halloween in Paradise
Treasure in Paradise
Fireworks in Paradise – *October 2017*
Beaches in Paradise – *June 2018*

Whales and Tails Cozy Mystery:

Romeow and Juliet
The Mad Catter
Grimm's Furry Tail
Much Ado About Felines
Legend of Tabby Hollow
Cat of Christmas Past
A Tale of Two Tabbies
The Great Catsby
Count Catula
The Cat of Christmas Present
A Winter's Tail
The Taming of the Tabby
Frankencat
The Cat of Christmas Future – *November 2017*
The Cat of New Orleans – *February 2018*

Seacliff High Mystery:

The Secret
The Curse
The Relic
The Conspiracy
The Grudge
The Shadow
The Haunting

Sand and Sea Hawaiian Mystery:

Murder at Dolphin Bay
Murder at Sunrise Beach
Murder at the Witching Hour
Murder at Christmas
Murder at Turtle Cove
Murder at Water's Edge
Murder at Midnight

Writers' Retreat Southern Mystery:

First Case
Second Look
Third Strike
Fourth Victim – *October 2017*
Fifth Night – *January 2018*

Rescue Alaska Paranormal Mystery:
Finding Justice – *November 2017*

A Tess and Tilly Mystery:
The Christmas Letter – *December 2017*

Road to Christmas Romance:
Road to Christmas Past

Chapter 1

Thursday, October 26

When is a broken watch found on the arm of a dead body a clue and when is it just a decoy? That was the question I'd been pondering since early this morning when I found the body of a man everyone thought had been dead for the past five years at the bottom of the bluff at Sunrise Beach.

"Earth to Lani," my cousin, roommate, and best friend Kekoa Pope said as she waved her hand in front of my face. We were sitting in the outdoor café at the Dolphin Bay Resort, where she worked in customer relations and I worked as a water safety officer.

I glanced at Kekoa and tried desperately to remember what she'd been rambling on about. "I'm sorry, what were we talking about?"

"The Halloween party next week and the awesome costume I just spent five minutes detailing. This body really has you preoccupied, which sort of surprises me. I'd think you'd be used to stumbling across bodies on the beach by now."

Kekoa had a point. I did seem to find more than my share of murder victims on or near the beach. "It's not that I found the body of a man at the bottom of the cliff that has me distracted; it's that the man I found has been dead for five years, yet he looked as if he couldn't have been dead for more than a few hours."

"They never did find the man's body five years ago. It seems obvious he didn't actually die when everyone thought he did."

"Perhaps," I acknowledged. "But my gut tells me otherwise."

Kekoa was about to respond when her phone rang. It was her boss, so she excused herself to take the call. That was fine by me because it gave me the opportunity to go over everything again in my mind.

Five years ago, my father, who's now retired but at the time had been an active detective for the Honolulu Police Department, had been investigating a series of homicides on the island and was pulling a late shift. He was heading home when a call came over the radio regarding the sound of a gunshot from a nearby oceanfront home. He just happened to be passing by the gated community, so he responded and discovered a woman lying dead on the floor in the master bedroom. My father had been able to respond within minutes of receiving the call, so he'd suspected the killer could still be close by. He called for backup and then went outside to look around. He was about to return to the murder scene when he saw a man running from the grounds out of the corner of his eye. He gave chase and, eventually, the men ended up at the edge of the bluff at Sunrise Beach. The man my dad was chasing must have realized he was trapped because he jumped from the bluff into the ocean. His body was never found, but my dad was certain the man couldn't have survived the fall into the rocky sea. It was assumed he'd been swept away by the strong tide the area was known for.

My father soon found out the female gunshot victim in the bedroom was Roxanne Bronwyn, an heiress who was famous for the parties she threw and the men she dated. During the investigation of the homicide, he'd learned Anastasia Cramer, a neighbor who lived two doors down from Bronwyn, had been reported missing by her sister after she failed to show up for a family reunion she was expected to attend. Although my father was a homicide detective and didn't usually investigate missing persons cases, he'd felt the two events could be related, so he'd gone to the Cramer home to look around. He'd found blood on the lanai that was confirmed to have belonged to her. He'd also found a photo of the man he'd seen jump into the sea, who'd turned out to be her husband, Clifford Cramer.

My father's investigation uncovered the fact that Mr. Cramer had been rumored to be having an affair with Bronwyn. When Mrs. Cramer never was found, it was assumed she must have found out about her husband's infidelity, confronted him, and for reasons no one was able to ascertain, he had killed her as well. Cramer was presumed dead after his leap into the sea and, after no further evidence turned up, the investigation had been shelved.

My father was never happy the case had been abandoned without solid proof of what had actually occurred, but there'd been a serial killer on the loose on the South Shore of Oahu, and his boss had wanted him to focus his energy on that more immediate case. The fact that Clifford Cramer's body had showed up at the bottom of the bluff at Sunrise Beach just this morning indicated to me that my father had been right to suspect the case wasn't as open and shut as assumed.

"Sorry about that," Kekoa said, sitting back down across from me. "He's been on a rampage lately, and because layoffs seem to be imminent, it's best to pacify him when I can."

"It's not a problem. I was just thinking about the implications of finding the body of a man who'd been considered to be dead for five years."

"I know it was quite a shock, but like I said before, the fact that you found his body sort of proves he didn't die when everyone thought he did," Kekoa pointed out.

She was probably correct, but my mind refused to accept the obvious answer as the only answer. "You've been to Sunrise Beach. There's very little chance a person could survive a fall onto the rocks at the bottom of the bluff even if it was high tide. And that's not all. Jason confirmed that the report Dad filed five years ago stated that the confrontation on the bluff took place at midnight. The watch on Cramer's arm was broken, the dial frozen at twelve o'clock."

"Maybe whoever killed him last night knew about the police report and staged things," Kekoa suggested.

I supposed it could have happened that way, but my imagination wouldn't quite let go of the idea that there was more to Clifford Cramer's death then met the eye.

"What are we talking about?" Our other roommate and Kekoa's current love interest, Cam Carrington, asked, as he joined us.

"We're talking about the likelihood of a man dying at the same time and place everyone thought he did five years earlier," Kekoa answered, after he gave her a quick kiss on the lips and sat down next to her.

"Maybe you should catch me up because so far, I'm lost," Cam, who was also a water safety officer at the resort, commented.

"I found a body at the bottom of the bluff at Sunrise Beach when I arrived to go surfing there this morning. It was early; the sun hadn't even risen over the horizon. The victim, I realized, was a man my dad saw jump from the bluff nearly five years ago. My mind tells me there's no way the man could have washed up on the beach five years after his death without showing any obvious signs of decay, but it appears that's exactly what happened."

"It seems a time warp or alien abduction are the only plausible explanations," Cam said in response to my story. "While they both seem feasible, I'm going to go with the man having been scooped up in a time warp five years ago and spit back out this morning."

"Cam's theory would explain a lot." I nodded.

"Sure, if this were a science fiction movie, but it isn't," Kekoa insisted. "In the current reality time warps don't exist, so the only plausible explanation is that Cramer didn't die five years ago and someone killed him last night. What does Jason think?"

Jason was the second oldest of my five brothers and a detective for the Honolulu Police Department.

He'd also been the first one to respond to my call that morning.

"He agrees with Kekoa that Clifford Cramer must not have died five years ago, but he did think it odd that the watch had stopped at twelve o'clock." I glanced at the waterproof watch on my arm. "Speaking of watches, I need to get back to my tower, but I'll see you both back at the condo after work. If you aren't busy maybe we can head to the beach."

"I'm in," Cam said.

"Yeah, me too," Kekoa seconded. "Is Luke still visiting his family in Texas?"

I nodded. My boyfriend, Luke Austin, had taken off for Texas without a moment's notice when his father was injured in a horseback riding accident. He'd asked his friend, Brody Waller, who lived in his pool house, to care for his dogs and horses until he returned. I thought it would be a quick trip, but he'd already been gone for more than three weeks. "Based on his last estimate he should be back next week as long as his father continues to improve."

"How *is* he doing?" Kekoa asked.

I let out a breath. "I'm not sure. Luke tries to put on a brave face whenever we Skype, but I can tell he's worried. He says his father gets a little stronger every day, but I get the feeling he's far from being able to return to his previous life."

"Do you think Luke will stay in Texas to help out with the ranch if his father doesn't improve?" Cam asked.

My stomach churned at the thought. "I don't know," I answered honestly. "Luke does have his horse ranch on Oahu to see to, but his family ranch in Texas is more than twenty times the size of Luke's enterprise. Luke has twelve horses while his dad has hundreds of cows. He does have two brothers who could help, but they each have their own ranches to deal with. Luke has said many times that he isn't interested in moving back to Texas, but I'm not certain he would turn his family down if they really needed him."

Kekoa gave my shoulder a squeeze. "There's absolutely no reason to worry about something that may never happen. I say we leave the stress of the day behind and head to the beach as you suggested."

"I'm all for some downtime. Let's bring some burgers and an ice chest full of beer. I'm off tomorrow, so I may as well enjoy the evening."

"Shredder is out of town, but maybe we can ask Sean and Kevin if they want to join us," Cam added.

Shredder, who'd never revealed his last name to us, Sean Trainor, and Kevin Green all lived in the same condominium we did.

"I'll call to ask them," I offered as I got up from my chair. "Brody is off today, but I'll call him as well."

Once I arrived at my tower I was updated on the current activity on the beach and water I'd been hired to protect by my boss, Mitch Hamilton, who'd taken over for me so I could have a break.

"A riptide warning is in place for the far south end of the beach," Mitch informed me. "So far, it hasn't been a problem, but you should keep an eye on it."

"Okay; anything else?"

"The group of surfers over near the jetty seems to have been drinking. I've already issued them several warnings about veering out of the surf zone into the swimming area. If they cause you any problems call security and we'll see about having them removed from the water. Other than that, it's been quiet. I did have one kid who cut his leg while climbing on the rocks, but I got him patched up."

"Thanks, Mitch. Will you be doing late-afternoon breaks as well?"

"Yeah." Mitch sighed. "Resort management wants me to cut my budget by twenty percent. The only way that's going to happen is if I spend some time on the sand."

"They still talking layoffs?"

Mitch nodded. "Laying people off is my least favorite part of my job."

"Maybe we can work it out so everyone gives up a few hours so no one has to lose their job. I'm currently on four tens. I'd be willing to go to four eights or three tens plus a short shift to give breaks until things pick up. If three of the others did that as well, one of the guards you'd otherwise have had to let go could stay on to cover the eight hours each of us donated to the cause."

"You'd do that?" Mitch looked surprised.

I shrugged. "Sure. To help out a friend. Jess is leaving at the end of the month anyway, so I'm assuming Makena is on the top of your cut list. I bet Cam and Brody would be all right with the idea if it meant she could stay on."

Mitch smiled. "I like the idea. I'll speak to Cam and Brody and, just to be fair, I'll make sure Drake agrees to the cut as well."

"Or, just another thought, you could fire Drake." Everyone knew Drake Longboard and I got along about as well as oil and water, but Mitch seemed to like him, so I doubted he'd end up on the chopping block no matter what happened.

It seemed like the cycle of layoffs followed by a mass hiring occurred every year. The summers were busy and then things dropped off in the fall, only to pick up again by Christmas. The resort management needed to figure out a better way of managing the employees if they wanted to attract and keep quality personnel.

"Excuse me, miss," a tall, thin woman with short blond hair said from the foot of my tower as Mitch walked away.

"How can I help you?"

"My son, Toby, is sure he saw a shark in the water."

I grabbed my binoculars. "Where?"

"Over near the group on that large yellow raft. He thinks you should make them get out at once."

I searched the area slowly, methodically looking for a fin, but didn't see anything even remotely alarming. I glanced back down at the woman. "Where's your son exactly?"

"Over there by the waterline. He's wearing dark blue swim trunks."

I glanced in the direction in which the woman was pointing. I'd seen the boy with the group on the raft earlier in the day. I grabbed my rescue can and jumped down from the tower. "I'm going to go talk to your son. If you could stay right here and listen for the radio, that would be great. If someone calls for me come and get me."

"Okay."

The woman looked worried, but I had a feeling the shark the boy said he saw was just a figment of his jealousy.

"Hi; my name's Lani," I introduced myself to the boy, who looked more angry than scared.

"Toby. Did my mom tell you about the shark?"

"She did. Can you tell me exactly what you saw?"

"I already told you, I saw a shark." The boy pointed into the distance. "Out near the group on the raft. You really should make them come in."

"Were you on the raft when you saw the shark?"

The boy shook his head. "They said they had too many people and I couldn't go."

"I see. Can you tell me exactly what you saw and where you were when you saw it?"

The boy looked back out toward the water. "I was standing here and I saw a fin. A big one."

"Was the fin you saw between the raft and the beach?" I asked.

"No, it was on the other side of the raft."

Based on the boy's location, as well as that of the raft, Toby would have needed binoculars to have seen a fin from that distance. "I bet you're mad at your friends for going out into the water and leaving you behind."

"Yeah."

"It doesn't seem quite fair. And I understand you might want to get them back for what they did, but reporting a fake shark sighting is a very bad thing to do and it could get someone in a lot of trouble. Are you sure you saw a shark?"

The boy looked scared, but I waited for his answer.

"I saw a shark. I did."

"Okay. Then I'll clear the water."

I grabbed my megaphone and instructed everyone in the water to return to the beach. I still didn't think Toby had really seen a shark, but I couldn't take the chance that he hadn't. Once everyone was out of the water I called Mitch, who said he'd check out the area with the rescue boat. If he cleared the area I'd allow the swimmers and surfers to reenter the water.

I climbed back onto my tower and scanned the water with my binoculars. By this point I sort of hoped there *was* a shark so the resort guests wouldn't be upset that we'd interrupted their day for nothing. You'd think our guests would want us to err on the side of caution, but more often than not that wasn't the case.

"See anything?" I asked Mitch over the two-way radio.

"Not yet. I'm going to do another sweep, but it looks like if there ever was a shark he's long gone."

"I'm pretty sure the shark was a ploy by a ten-year-old to get back at his friends for not letting him join them on the raft."

Mitch chuckled. "Smart kid. There's no way for us to prove or disprove what he said he saw as long as he keeps to his story. Hang on; I see something in the water up ahead."

I waited for Mitch to get back to me.

"Close the beach and call HPD. The thing I saw in the water was an arm."

Chapter 2

Cam and I had the beach cleared by the time Jason and his partner, Colin, showed up. Mitch had retrieved the arm and had it waiting back at lifeguard headquarters. I had no idea if one of the swimmers or surfers had been attacked without anyone noticing—very unlikely—or if the arm had drifted toward the beach from another location. The really strange thing was, once Mitch found the arm, Toby backtracked and said he'd made the whole thing up.

"So, what do you think?" Mitch asked Jason when we'd all gathered in his office.

"The arm has been in the water for a while," Jason answered. "I'm going to say at least ten or twelve hours."

"What are the odds some kid would report a fake shark sighting only to have the fake report lead to the actual retrieval of a human body part?" Cam asked. "The whole thing is too absurd."

Jason, who was wearing a pair of gloves, turned the arm and the attached hand to the side. "It looks as if it belonged to a female. Probably middle-aged. The hand is intact, so we should be able to pull prints. Hopefully, there will be something in the database to match them to."

"Do you think this arm is related to the dead body I found on the beach this morning?" I asked.

"I would say that's very likely," Jason answered. "I have a couple of men in boats looking for additional remains. I'll need you to keep the beach closed and the water clear for the remainder of the day."

"It's not going to be easy," I commented.

"I have a feeling once the shark attack story gets around folks will be willing to comply," Jason reasoned.

I returned to the beach to post signs letting the resort guests know the beach and water would be closed for the remainder of the day, but they were welcome to use one of the three resort pools. Mitch wanted me to patrol the beach for a couple of hours while Jason's men did their thing, so although there was no one in the water or on the sand to watch, I still hadn't been released to go home.

I decided to use the downtime to call Luke and fill him in on my very eventful day. The problem was, he didn't answer. I left a message and called Brody.

"Hey, Brody, it's Lani."

"Hey, girl. What's up?"

"Dead man on the beach this morning and a severed arm in the water this afternoon. Other than that, not a lot."

"What?"

"Oh, and it gets better," I added. "The body I found on the beach this morning belongs to a man who's been dead for the past five years. At least everyone *thought* he was dead. Given the fact that the body hadn't decayed in the least, I'm going to guess everyone was wrong, unless Cam's idea about a time warp turns out to be valid."

Brody was silent for a moment before he replied, "Are you pulling my leg? Is this a prank of some sort, or maybe payback for the dead fish I left in your locker a while back?"

"That was you? I assumed it was Drake. Why would you do such a thing?"

"You know boys and dares."

I groaned. "I almost got fired when I retaliated by putting a dirty diaper I found in the bathroom in Drake's locker. I can't believe it was you the whole time."

"Yeah, I felt bad about that. But enough about that; did you really find a severed arm?"

"Mitch did, while checking out a fake shark report. Jason doesn't think the arm was severed from a body as the result of a shark attack, however. Maybe Cam is right. Maybe we *are* in some sort of a time warp or alternate dimension, because a lot of really weird stuff is happening."

Brody chuckled. "Leave it to you to get wrapped up in another stranger-than-strange mystery."

"Yeah, lucky me. Listen, have you heard from Luke lately?" I asked, steering the conversation toward the real reason for my call.

"Yeah, I spoke to him this morning. Why?"

"I keep missing him, so we haven't talked for a few days. How did he seem?"

"Seem?"

"Was he still worried about his dad or did it seem as if things were getting better?"

"I don't know. We didn't talk about his dad or his feelings. He called to let me know that a buyer was coming by to look at two of the horses this afternoon. He wanted to be sure I'd be here and he gave me instructions on what to say and what not to say while the man's here."

I frowned. "He's selling two more horses? Doesn't that make six since he's been gone?"

"Yeah. So?" Brody asked. "He's a horse breeder. He breeds and sells horses for a living."

"I know that, but I've never known him to sell so many horses in such a short time. Are you sure he didn't say anything about how things are going with his dad?"

"I'm sure. If you want to know how things are why don't you call him and ask?"

I bit my lip as I stared out at the empty water. "Yeah, I will. Did Luke happen to say when he'd be back?"

"I don't think he knows for sure yet. He asked if I was doing okay handling the animals on my own and I assured him I was. I told him to take the time he needed and he thanked me. While he didn't specifically mention his dad, I got the impression things were pretty bad. Poor guy seemed to have a lot to deal with, if you know what I mean."

I took a deep breath and tried to calm the feeling of dread in the pit of my stomach. "I know. I'll call him later. But if he calls you again and if you get any interesting news will you call me?"

"Sure. Okay." Brody paused. "Are things okay between you and Luke?"

"I don't know. I've left messages he hasn't returned, and when we do connect our conversations are short and he seems eager to get off the phone. I know he's dealing with a lot and I don't want to seem needy, but if I'm honest with myself, I'm starting to feel a little needy."

"I'm sure Luke's just worried about his dad. Everything will be fine once he gets home," Brody assured me.

"I hope so. By the way, before I forget, Cam, Kekoa, and I are going to the beach after work. Burgers, beer, and surfing. You in?"

"Totally."

"I'm bringing Sandy," I said, referring to my dog. "You should bring Duke and Dallas," I added, naming Luke's dogs. "It's been a while since they've had a chance to hang out."

"I'll do that. We going to the usual spot?"

"Depends on the waves. I'll text you once we settle on a location."

After I hung up with Brody I called Luke again. Still no answer. I'd already left a message, so there was no use leaving another. I decided I needed to burn off some energy. I was supposed to keep people off the beach, but there was no one in the water to keep an eye on, so I jogged up and down the shore while I waited for Mitch to tell me it was okay to leave.

******

The waves that evening weren't great, but they were acceptable, and the food and conversation were excellent. I found myself beginning to relax and have fun. There's a saying that the worst day on the water is still better than the best day anywhere else, and most of the time I found I agreed. The days were getting shorter, so the sun had already begun its descent beyond the horizon when Brody showed up with Duke and Dallas. As I watched the dogs greet each other with doggy enthusiasm, it hit me how very much I missed Luke. He'd called me back while I was in the shower and left a message letting me know he was going to his sister's for dinner and he'd try to catch up with me the following day. I wanted to call him and beg him to call me when he got back to his parents', no matter how late it was, but again I found myself feeling needy and emotional, which wasn't something I cared for at all.

"Why the long face?" Brody asked after I'd paddled in and joined the group by the fire.

I forced a smile as I wrung water out of my long hair. "I guess I'm just tired. It's been a long day. I'm glad I have tomorrow off. Did Mitch call you about my idea to save Makena's job?"

"Makena's job needs saving?"

I explained my idea about all the four WSOs— me, him, Cam, and Drake—donating eight of our forty hours a week to give up enough hours to cover the job for Makena, the most recent hire, so Mitch wouldn't need to cut the twenty percent staff now that Jess was leaving anyway.

"That sounds like an excellent plan, but I think I may take a leave anyway, which would mean Makena could stay on in my place."

"You're taking a leave? Why?"

"I spoke to Luke again this afternoon after the guy came to look at the horses. He asked if I'd be interested in signing on with him as a ranch hand. Living for free in his pool house means my expenses are minimal, but he figured he could use the full-time help. He offered to pay me to manage the property while he's away."

My heart sank. "So, he's going to be gone longer than he expected."

Brody squeezed my hand. "Yeah. It sounded to me as if his stay in Texas was going to be indefinite. He mentioned that his dad is going to be coming home from the hospital in a couple of days, but there's no way he can run the ranch. They have reliable long-term employees, but Luke said his dad was nervous about not having any oversight. I could tell he was conflicted, but I also sensed he was willing to do whatever it took to put his mom and dad at ease."

I suppressed the tears that threatened to spill down my face. "I guess it makes sense for Luke to put his parents' needs before his own. He's a good son."

Brody put his arm around my shoulders. "I know this is hard on him, but he's the sort of man to put his family first."

"Do you think he's ever coming back?"

Brody paused before answering. "I think so. If he wasn't I figure he'd sell the rest of his livestock rather than paying me to keep an eye on the place."

I supposed Brody had a point. If Luke was definitely staying in Texas it would make the most sense to cash out.

"Thanks for letting me know," I said. "When he springs it on me tomorrow I'll be prepared."

"I'm going to go take a final run before it gets totally dark," Brody informed me. "Want to come?"

I shrugged. "Yeah. I have some energy to burn."

******

When the phone rang later, after we'd returned home, I hoped it was Luke, but it was Jason.

"Hey, Jas, what's up?" I asked as I sat on the chaise on the lanai overlooking the ocean, pondering the emptiness in my heart.

"I have news I thought you'd be interested in."

"Okay, shoot." I certainly could use some good or even just interesting news at that point.

"First, both Clifford Cramer's body and the arm we found—which happened to have belonged to Anastasia Cramer—had been previously frozen."

I frowned. "So Cramer and his wife both did die five years ago but someone froze them?"

"We can't know for certain when they died yet, or how long they've been frozen, but it seems likely they've been dead since Mrs. Cramer went missing and Mr. Cramer jumped from the bluff."

"But Cramer's wife was reported missing the day before he jumped from the bluff. It was assumed he killed her. Do you think he was the one to put her on ice? And if he was, who put *him* on ice?"

"Both good and unanswered questions."

"Are you reopening both cases?"

"HPD is taking another look, although I won't be assigned to the case. They want me to continue to focus on more recent murders unless something relevant surfaces in the Cramer case. For the time being, the case has been assigned to a rookie. Given the fact that it won't be my toes you're stepping on but someone who's out to prove themselves and won't take kindly to interference, I'm suggesting you sit this one out."

I let out a long breath. "Yeah, okay. I understand, but I'm curious why after five years of being frozen both bodies were dumped into the ocean. I mean, why now? Is there some link between those cases and something going on right now?"

I heard Jason groan. "You aren't going to leave this alone, are you?"

"You know how I get. Sometimes I can't help myself. There are just so many unanswered questions. Who killed Anastasia Cramer? Was it her husband, as Dad assumed, or someone else? And when did she die? It was thought when she never turned up after her sister reported her missing that he killed and buried her before he died, but did he? Or did someone else actually kill and freeze her? And how did Clifford Cramer end up frozen as well? Did the person who froze him find him floating in the ocean after he jumped from the bluff, or did he survive the fall after all, only to have someone kill and freeze him at some later point? And then there's the timing of both bodies ending up in the water today. Who put them in the water and why? Have they been on ice for five years, or were they somewhere else and they died more recently?"

Jason paused and then replied, "So you really aren't going to leave this alone?"

"I'm not sure I can."

"I used to think having you on the force was a bad idea, but now I think it may be the only way to keep you out of trouble. They're selecting names next week for the next academy class, which I believe starts in a month or so. If you promise to sit this one out I'll put in a good word for you."

I grinned. "Really? You would do that?"

"I've been thinking about it anyway. You seem to have matured lately. I think you're ready."

"You're damn right I'm ready." Suddenly my mood had improved quite a bit.

"So, do you think you can stay out of the way of the rookie assigned to the Cramer case?"

"I will. And thanks, Jason. For everything."

I won't say my day had turned into the best one ever, but I did feel better than I had. I knew in my heart that if I was patient, things would work out the way I'd always dreamed.

Chapter 3

Friday, October 27

Luke called before I'd even gotten out of bed this morning, but I didn't care in the least that my sleep had been interrupted. I was just happy to hear his voice after tossing and turning all night, wondering if we had a future together or if all we'd ever have was the past.

"I'm so glad you called. I've missed you," I said.

"I've missed you too. More than you know."

I sat up and leaned against my pillows. "How's your dad?"

Luke sighed. "Not good. He's alive and he doesn't have any life-threatening injuries, but he isn't able to get around on his own and he seems to be in pain a good deal of the time. I hoped to be home by now, but I don't feel like I can just desert my mom when she needs me."

"I understand. I really do. And I'm so sorry your family has had to go through such a difficult ordeal."

Luke didn't answer right away and I found myself grasping for something to say that would make the conversation less awkward. "I spoke to Jason last night. He told me that he's going to put in a good word with the academy review committee for me. There's a class starting in a month and if all goes according to plan, I should finally get my shot."

"That's wonderful, Lani. I'm happy for you." While Luke's words sounded happy his tone was flat.

"I won't have the official invite for a couple of weeks, but once I do we'll go out and celebrate. I can't believe after a lifetime of hoping and planning I might actually get my shot."

"I'm very proud of you and we'll celebrate." Luke sounded tired. "When I get back."

"Do you have any idea when that might be?"

He sighed. "I'm not sure. We were planning to have a Halloween party at my place. When we talked about it I was certain I'd be back, but now it looks like I'll have to miss it. I want you to use the house, though. I know the invitations have all been sent and you have a lot of people planning to come. You have a key and Brody can help you with anything you need."

I tried to keep the panic out of my voice. Luke had enough to deal with without having to worry about me. "Thank you. I appreciate that. I really hope you can make the trip home, but I understand if you can't. I'm off today, so I'll probably buy some decorations and go by to begin decorating. If that's okay…"

"That's perfectly fine. Brody is seeing to the animals, but feel free to stay at the house if you want to. I realize things have become a bit more awkward at the condo now that Cam and Kekoa have hooked up."

"Things here are okay, but I may take you up on your offer. I know Sandy misses hanging out with Duke and Dallas. I bet they miss you as well. Even if you can't come home permanently yet, perhaps you can manage a short visit?"

Luke didn't answer right away, but I could hear someone talking in the background, so I imagined his focus was divided. After a short pause he came back on the line. "I'm sorry; I have to go."

"Okay. Will you call me later?"

"I'll try. It might be late."

"Any time is fine. Really."

"Okay. I love you."

"I love you too."

I sat and stared at the phone after Luke hung up. He sounded so tired and sort of defeated.

Sandy jumped onto the bed. He seemed to understand I was sad because he put his paw on my stomach and cuddled his head up against my face. I put my arms around him and cried the tears I'd been holding at bay. I didn't know what I was going to do if Luke and I were over. I'd finally gotten to the point where I'd begun to think I might be ready for the next step in our relationship. Luke had mentioned my moving in with him on several occasions, but until recently I'd felt I wasn't ready. Maybe my subconscious had known things were going to get difficult and had warned me to wait rather than jumping in.

I cried myself out, then got up and took a warm shower. Agonizing over Luke and what may or may not occur in the future wasn't going to make a bit of difference to the eventual outcome.

"Morning," I said to Kekoa, who was sitting at the dining table drinking coffee. "Are you going in late today?"

"I'm off. One of the other girls wanted to trade for two Saturdays from now and I figured a day off in the middle of the week would be nice, so I agreed. What's wrong?"

"Nothing." I tried for a smile even I knew was flat.

"No. It's not nothing. We've been best friends since we were in diapers. I know when something's wrong. Spill."

I poured myself a cup of coffee and sat down at the table. Kekoa was waiting patiently for me to reply, but her patience only extended so far. I took a sip of my coffee and then tried to find the words to satisfy her without breaking down again.

"I spoke to Luke this morning," I began. "I was happy to hear from him, but hearing his voice reminded me how much I miss him. I guess I'm just feeling a little sad."

Kekoa tilted her head as she studied my face. I turned away. "No," she said. "It's more than that. I realize you miss Luke and I understand that makes you sad, but I'm sensing something else."

"I promise there's nothing else." I couldn't quite make myself look Kekoa in the eye when I said it and that was going to come back to bite me.

"You're lying," Kekoa challenged. "We made a pinky swear in the first grade never to lie to each other, so what gives?"

I took a deep breath, clenching my fist as I fought for control. "Look, I know you mean well, but I didn't sleep well last night and I'm really not up for an interrogation. My boyfriend has been gone for over three weeks with no immediate plans to return and I miss him. That's the end of the story."

"Anger," Kekoa said. "The emotion you don't want me to know about is anger."

Damn.

"Are you angry with Luke?" Kekoa asked.

"Of course I'm angry with Luke. And I'm angry with myself too. I feel like such an idiot. I knew from the very first moment I met Luke that he'd eventually go back to Texas, but I let him get under my skin anyway. I let him love me and I let myself fall in love with him. I'm such an idiot."

Kekoa knelt on the floor in front of me. She gathered me into her arms for a tight hug. I thought I'd cried out all my anger, fear, and pain that morning, but apparently, I was wrong. After a while I pulled myself together and Kekoa handed me a tissue.

"Feel better?" she asked.

I nodded. "Actually, I do. Until you forced it out of me, I didn't even realize I was angry. What does that say about me?"

"It says you're human. It says you're suddenly in a position where you see your biggest fear confronting you and you don't know how to handle it."

"But Luke's father has been injured and his life will never be the same. I must be a horrible person to try to make this all about me."

Kekoa placed her hand over mine. "You aren't horrible. You're scared, and fear can make you angry.

It's a natural progression. The more scared you are, the angrier you become."

Kekoa was right. I'd been scared about this very thing since I first let Luke into my life, but I'd chosen to push it to the back of my mind. The longer Luke had been gone, the more scared I'd become until all that fear had turned into anger. "What should I do?"

Kekoa didn't answer immediately. Finally, she said, "I don't know. I understand your fear and your anger, and normally, I'd say you should talk to Luke about it, but he has a lot on his plate already. It's not like he's on vacation. I'm sure he doesn't want to be away any more than you want him to, but he's doing what needs to be done. I admire him for that.'

"Yeah." I sighed. "I do too. And I don't want to make this harder for him." I squeezed Kekoa's hand with mine. "Thanks. I do feel better. Maybe I just needed to acknowledge my feelings."

"I'm glad I could help. How about we do something fun because we both have the day off? I could use a girls' day."

"I planned to go shopping for Halloween decorations today. Do you want to come with me?"

"Sounds like fun. Are you still planning to have the party at Luke's house with everything that's happened?"

I nodded. "He said he was fine with it even if he doesn't make it home. In fact, he said I could stay at his place if I wanted to. I might do that. At least until after the party."

Kekoa frowned. "Are you sure? Won't you be lonely? Won't it make it harder to be in his home when he isn't there?"

I shrugged. "Maybe. I just figured his house is empty and you and Cam could probably use some privacy."

Kekoa got up and poured us each a second cup of coffee. "This is your home. Neither Cam nor I want things to be awkward for you."

"I know. This may sound strange, but I think being in Luke's home, sleeping in his bed, and helping Brody with the animals will make me feel closer to him. At the very least I think it will help me to feel I'm doing what I can to help him. Sitting on the sidelines while he has to deal with this extremely difficult situation has been frustrating for me. Maybe if I feel like I'm part of the solution I won't feel quite so bad."

"Okay. If you're sure that's what you want to do I think you should." Kekoa stood up. "Let me grab a shower and then we can go shopping. I might get a few things to decorate the condo as well."

******

We decided to head toward the south shore, where there were more shopping options. We figured as long as we were both off we'd make a day of it. We'd buy the decorations, have some lunch, and she could even help me find the perfect costume. The first stop we made was to the Halloween Store. We filled our basket with black and orange streamers, black and orange balloons, small orange and white lights, a mechanical monster, and even a fog machine. It would be fun to decorate the patio area and pool. Halloween in Hawaii tended to be warm, much like every other holiday.

"Check out these little ghosts." Kekoa held up some glow-in-the-dark ghosts strung on a line. "They have white, green, and purple. We could buy some of each color and wrap them in the shrubs at the end of the patio. It'll look like they're invading once all the lights are off."

"Grab a couple packs of each color," I said. "I saw some packages of webbing. We can string that around the house with some of those plastic spiders."

"Should we get one of these coffins to serve the food out of?"

I walked over to where Kekoa was standing. "It's really awesome, but it's kind of big. I'm not sure we could even get it home. We could get one of these tubs for the drinks." Kekoa picked up some paper cups and I was about to add some cute paper plates to the basket when my phone rang. I looked at the caller ID. "It's Jason. I should get this."

"You might want to take it outside," Kekoa suggested. "I'll get in line."

I did as Kekoa suggested and stepped out into the warm sunshine. "Hey, Jason. What's up?"

"I'm going to follow up on some leads regarding the Cramer case this afternoon, but I wanted to ask you a few questions first."

"I thought it was being investigated by a rookie."

"Yeah, well, this rookie is a lot greener than I'd like. I spoke to Dad last night and he told me some stuff that got me thinking. I decided to take a look myself."

I sat down on a brick wall under a tree. "Okay; shoot."

"When you discovered Clifford Cramer's body at the bottom of the bluff was the tide on its way in or out?"

"Out. The body was mostly covered with water when I first arrived, although by the time you got there the body was completely exposed."

"Did you notice anything in the water near the body?"

I paused to consider Jason's question. "I saw several plastic bags floating on the surface of the water, but they were quite a way out. In fact, the reason I went over to the rocks at the base of the bluff in the first place was because of the bags. I know plastic can be dangerous to sea life, so I was going to swim out and grab them when I saw the body."

"I don't remember seeing plastic bags in the surf," Jason commented.

I furrowed my brow as I tried to remember. "They were gone by the time you arrived. You know how strong the current is in that area. The tide started back out and took whatever was in the water with it. I remember thinking that if the body hadn't been tangled up in the rocks the way it was, it would have been washed out to sea as well. Is there a specific reason you're asking about items floating in the water?"

Jason hesitated. "Maybe. I have a hunch. I know you said the bags were pretty far out, but can you describe them? Were they large or small, heavy-duty or lightweight, colored or clear?"

"They were black. And large. I'd say they were the size of liners used for a small indoor trash can. Those bags looked sturdier than trash bags, though."

"Did it seem as if they were waterproof?"

"I don't know. Maybe. Like I said, they were floating out to sea by the time I got there."

"Did they appear to be empty or did it seem they contained something?"

"If I had to guess they were empty. They were just floating on top of the water. It didn't seem like anything was weighing them down."

"And how many were there?"

"Maybe eight or ten. Why all the questions about the bags?"

"Just following a hunch. Did you see anything else?"

"There was something shiny. I'm not sure what. Maybe a fishing lure? It could have been something else. To be honest, once I realized the thing I saw between the rocks was a body I stopped looking at the water."

"That's understandable."

"What about Mrs. Cramer? Do you think she was dumped in the same area Mr. Cramer was?" I asked.

Jason cleared his throat, then answered. "We aren't sure. Based on the location Cramer's body was found and the tides, we have a general idea as to where he would have entered the water. And based on where the arm was found, combined with the tide pattern around Dolphin Bay Resort, we believe Mrs. Cramer's body entered the water from a different location altogether. Either that or a shark severed her arm from her body and dragged her for some distance before the arm detached, which put it in a different current, heading away from the bluff."

"I'm going to put my money on the shark theory. It would be strange for one person to dispose of two bodies in different locations."

"I agree. It would seem logical to dump both bodies at the same time. Listen, I need to get going. I'll catch up with you later."

"Okay. I hope I was able to help. Kekoa and I are on the south shore shopping, but if I can help in any other way just let me know."

After I hung up I went back into the store. Although the place was packed, Kekoa had managed to make it to the front of the line.

"Maybe we should have bowls of candy sitting around," Kekoa suggested. "I mean, it's a Halloween party."

I picked up two cute pumpkin bowls. "We can get candy when we get the food. Let's head to lunch after this. I'm starving."

"Okay. I could eat. Did Jason have news?"

"More like questions."

"Did you help him?"

"Maybe. I feel like he has a theory he's trying to verify. I guess my answer to his question either verified his suspicion or not."

Chapter 4

After Kekoa and I finished our shopping we headed out to Luke's to drop everything off. Duke and Dallas seemed happy to see me and I thought about staying, but it was late and I didn't have Sandy with me, so I decided to go back to the condo with Kekoa and maybe spend the night at Luke's the following evening. It was only a few days until the party, so I had to jump on the decorating sooner rather than later. I was off on Sundays and Mondays and the party was on Tuesday, so I could do whatever still needed to be done while I was off.

When Kekoa and I arrived at the condo my brother Jeff was sitting on the lanai. He was the youngest of my five brothers and closest to me in age, which meant that growing up I was much closer to him than I was to the others. Even given that, I was surprised to see him sitting in the swing Kekoa and I had gone in on together that summer. Jeff, who was Mom's favorite of the boys and the most spoiled of all my brothers, lived on Maui and worked as an officer for their police department. He'd gotten married over a year ago and, since that time, hadn't visited me even once at the condo.

"Jeff." I set my purse down and hugged him. "What are you doing here?"

Jeff hesitated before answering. It was then I noticed the look on his face, and my stomach sank.

"Oh God. What's happened?" I demanded.

"It's Jason."

I put a hand to my chest to keep my heart from pounding its way clean through. "What happened to him?"

"He's been shot."

Now I was pretty sure my heart had stopped beating altogether. "Is he…?" I wanted to ask if he was dead, but I couldn't quite get the words out.

"He's in surgery."

I glanced at Kekoa, who had tears running down her face. "I have to go. Will you take care of Sandy?"

She nodded. I could see she was fighting for control.

I let Jeff lead me to his car. I don't remember anything about the ride to the hospital. Maybe we talked, maybe we didn't. Looking back, I must have been in shock because all I remember was feeling numb. When we entered the waiting area we found my oldest brother, John, a detective for the Maui PD, and my second youngest brother, Justin, a street cop for the Honolulu PD, sitting on brown sofas. John stood up and I walked into his arms. Because he was the oldest I'd lived with him for the shortest time. He was already fourteen when I was born, so by the time I remember hanging out with my other brothers, he'd already moved out. Still, when I was hurting or in trouble, he was the one I was most likely to run to.

I'm not sure if it was because he was the oldest, or if it was because he was the largest physically, but when he put his arms around me he had a way of letting me know he'd take care of things and everything would work out fine.

"Have you heard anything?" I asked as John tightened his arms around me.

"Not yet."

"Jimmy?" Jimmy was the middle brother, the jokester of the group, and a cop on Kauai.

"On his way. Let's sit down. I think it's going to be a long night."

I sat down next to John and looked around the room. There were a few people milling around, but other than us, the room was mostly empty. "Where are Mom and Dad?"

"With the kids," John answered. He was referring to Kala and Kale, Jason's daughter and son.

John put his arm around my shoulders and I rested my head on his arm. When he spoke it was in a soft, even manner. "I offered to stay with them until Alana's sister got here, but they were hysterical and wanted Grandpa and Grandma."

"And Alana?" I asked, realizing for the first time that Jason's wife wasn't in the room.

"She's with her parents in the chapel. As you would expect, she's taking this really hard."

I felt so helpless, just sitting there doing nothing, and was about to volunteer to go sit with Kala and Kale when my parents walked in. I stood up and my mother walked into my arms. I glanced over her shoulder at my dad, who looked about as lost and forlorn as I'd ever seen him.

"Is Alana's sister with the kids?" I asked my mom, as my brothers moved farther apart, making room for Mom and me between John and Jeff.

"Yes," Mom answered as Dad stepped into the hallway to make a call.

"How are they holding up?" I knew the answer but felt I should ask.

"They were pretty hysterical, but I managed to get them to sleep before we left. I thought Alana would be here."

"In the chapel with her parents," I answered. I glanced at Dad, who was pacing back and forth, talking on his phone. "Who's Dad talking to?"

Mom folded her hands in her lap and looked off into the distance. "I don't know. He's been on the phone since we heard. He's trying to find out who shot Jason."

"You mean they don't know?"

Mom shook her head. Tears streamed down her cheeks. "He didn't tell anyone where he was going when he left the precinct. Someone found him in an alley and called it in. As of the last I heard, no one knew why he was anywhere near where he was found or who might have put a bullet in his chest."

I glanced at Justin. Being five years younger than Jason, he often expressed his discontent with his role in Jason's shadow because both worked for HPD, but I knew in some small space in his mind he was probably blaming himself. That's what we Pope kids tended to do: blame ourselves for things that were completely out of our control. Of course I know there's no way Justin could have known what was going on or what would happen, but, of all my brothers, he was the one who tended to be hardest on himself.

"Do you know anything at all?" I asked.

Justin shook his head. "I knew Jason had some questions regarding the body you found, but he never said a word to anyone about where he was going."

"He called me," I said. "Earlier, around lunchtime."

Justin sat forward. "What did he want?"

"He asked me about Clifford Cramer. The man I found on the beach. He wanted to know if the tide was going in or out when I found him, and he asked if there was anything else in the water."

Justin took my hand and led me out to the hallway. When we were alone he asked me to repeat everything Jason had asked and everything I'd told him. I mentioned the shiny thing in the water, as well as the plastic bags. There wasn't a lot to tell, and that information on its own didn't mean anything.

Justin and I were about to rejoin the others when Jimmy arrived. The three of us walked back into the waiting room together to find Alana and her parents were with the others. I'm not sure how to describe the next several hours other than to call them pure hell. Each minute that ticked by without a word as to whether Jason would live or die was more than any of us could bear. Alana was pale as a sheet and my mother looked like she was aging before my eyes. Dad was on and off the phone, as was Justin, while Jimmy and Jeff tried to keep Mom from falling apart completely and John wandered the halls, trying to find someone who could give us an update.

After a while I got tired of sitting and went out into the hallway to track down my dad. "Did you find out anything?" I asked.

Dad just shook his head. I had never seen him look so defeated.

"I spoke to Jason this afternoon. Around lunchtime."

Dad narrowed his gaze. "What about?"

I told him what I'd told Justin about the tide and the items in the water. "I know you investigated Cramer five years ago. Does any of that mean anything to you?"

He took several deep breaths before leaning against the wall. I could see he was deep in thought. Finally, he spoke. "You said you saw plastic bags in the water?"

"There were several."

"Were they grocery bags or watertight ones with a seal?"

"They looked heavy-duty. I didn't actually get a close look at them, but my guess is if they were sealed they could be watertight."

"Large or small?"

"Large. They were as big as a liner for a small home trash can." I watched my father's face. "Does that mean anything to you?"

"I'm not sure. What I do know is that for Jason to take off in the middle of the day and not tell anyone where he was going, it must have meant something to him. I intend to find out what it was."

"Let me help you." I could see Dad was about to refuse and expected as much, but instead he said, "Let's talk about this tomorrow. For now, we should be with the family."

******

"Here comes the doctor," Jeff said two hours later.

We all stood up, waiting. It was hard to tell by the look on his face what sort of news he had. He wasn't frowning, but he wasn't smiling either. When he reached us Alana stepped forward.

"How is he?" she asked.

"Alive."

I could see her physically relax just a bit.

"The bullet was fired from a fairly close range. Luckily, it didn't damage any important organs before becoming lodged in his spine. We managed to extract the bullet, but your husband lost a lot of blood. At this point all we can do is wait. The next twenty-four hours will tell us a lot."

"Can I see him?" Alana asked.

"For a minute, but only you." The doctor looked at the rest of us. "Go home. Get some rest. Detective Pope won't regain consciousness for quite some time."

"You said the bullet lodged in his spine. Will he have spinal damage?" John asked.

"He may."

"Will he be able to walk?" I asked.

"It's too early to tell. I'm going to suggest again that you all get some rest. We should know more tomorrow."

Justin lived on Oahu, as did I. Jeff, John, and Jimmy all went home with Mom and Dad. Alana and the kids would go to my parents' as well because there would be a lot of people on hand to help take care of the kids. Alana's parents weren't in the best of health and her sister had four children of her own.

I hadn't slept in my childhood room in years, but that night I wanted to be with my family. Mom had kept all our bedrooms just as they were when we moved out, so I grabbed Sandy and an overnight bag and headed in that direction. My parents had a foster child, Tommy, who had taken over the room we'd used as a den when I was growing up. It would have made sense for Mom to let him use one of our rooms because we'd all moved out, but she insisted our rooms were our rooms and always would be. In the end, I guess it worked out. Tommy was visiting a friend for the weekend, so Alana was in Jason's old room and Kala and Kale were in Tommy's room.

After my parents, Alana, and the kids had all gone to bed, my four brothers and I sat around the dining room table nursing beers. It had been such a long day, but I was still wound up. I could see they were as well.

"Are you sure you should have that second beer?" John, always the responsible one, asked Justin. "You need to drive home."

Justin popped the lid. "I'll just stay here."

I understood where Justin was coming from. He only lived a few miles away, but tonight there was comfort in company.

"Can you all stay?" I asked my brothers.

"I took a few days of my vacation time when I heard," John informed us. "I'll take more if I need to."

"I took a couple of days as well," Jimmy answered.

"I have the next two days off anyway," Jeff said. "After that, if things are still uncertain, I'll take a leave for as long as I'm needed, although I hate to leave Candy alone for too long."

I looked at Justin. He shrugged. "I might be better off on duty. You know Dad is making plans to launch his own unofficial investigation. I think it will be important for me to be at the station, where I can keep an eye on things."

"I'm not sure Dad getting involved is the best idea," John said. "He's getting on in years and he isn't a cop any longer. I'd hate for this to backfire on him and make things worse. I'm sure HPD are on it and don't need his help."

"He can be pretty stubborn," Justin reminded John.

"I'll talk to him," he offered.

"Be firm," Jimmy said.

"You need to convince Dad to let his sons handle this," Justin added.

"Hey, what about me?" I asked.

"You aren't a cop," John pointed out.

"Not yet. But I can help."

Jimmy tugged one of my pigtails like he had when I was a kid. "No need to worry your pretty little head. You stay here and help Mom with the kids while your big brothers take care of the monster who shot Jason."

Like hell!

Chapter 5

Saturday, October 28

The next morning the family gathered for breakfast. Mom, who often used cooking as a means of stress relief, had gone all out, making SPAM, rice, eggs, and biscuits. Based on the huge platters of food, she must have gotten up really early and headed directly to the kitchen.

"It seems we should have heard something by now," John stated as he filled his plate for the second time.

Mom gave John a meaningful glance as she nodded toward Kale and Kala. Alana didn't want to upset them more than they already were.

"I'm sure Jason is just sleeping in," Dad commented before getting up and heading to his office.

"Can we see Daddy today?" Kala asked.

"I think your dad has a lot of visitors already lining up to see him," Mom replied. "How about if we make him some of his favorite cookies for when he's feeling better?"

Both kids seemed to think that was a fine idea. Jimmy jumped in with a funny story about a fishing trip gone horribly wrong, which further distracted them while we finished our meal. Once they'd finished eating the kids were excused to go watch cartoons. As soon as they left the room, the adults began to discuss the subject on everyone's mind. While we were all worried about Jason, the Popes were a cop family, and finding the man who had the nerve to shoot a cop and bringing him to justice was at the forefront of our minds.

My brothers all seemed to have ideas about how to proceed, but in my opinion none of them were any more relevant than the others. I was still angry that they'd decided not to include me in their theory building, but I didn't want to start an argument, so I sat quietly and ate my food until Dad eventually returned to the table.

"I spoke to Jason's doctor," he informed us after retaking his seat at the head of the table. "He's still in intensive care and hasn't regained consciousness, but his vitals have stabilized. The doctor assured me Jason's prognosis is a lot more promising than it seemed when he spoke to us last night."

"That's great," I said. "Can we see him?"

"The only visitors they're allowing right now are Alana, Mom, and me." Dad looked at John. "They're only allowing two visitors this morning, so I wondered if you could drive Alana and your mother. I have some leads I need to follow up on."

John frowned but agreed. I wasn't sure whether he'd gotten around to speaking to Dad about letting his sons handle things; based on this conversation, I assumed not.

John left with Mom and Alana, and Dad took off too, I assumed to follow up on the leads he'd referred to. Justin went to work, and Jimmy, Jeff, and I were assigned to stay with Kale and Kala. Jimmy and Jeff were a good distraction for the kids and spent most of the morning wrestling around like they did when they were Kale and Kala's age. As the middle son, Jimmy had taken on the role of peacemaker between his older brothers, who tended to be serious, and his younger ones, who were still young enough to want to have some fun. Jimmy tended to be a goofball, but at times like these his playful personality was a welcome relief from the very real drama playing out in the background.

A couple of hours later Dad returned and went directly to his office. Shortly after that, John brought Mom home, although Alana decided to stay at the hospital. Mom headed into the kitchen with Kala and Kale to make cookies for their father, John joined Dad in his office, and Jimmy and Jeff went into town to meet up with Justin. Everyone was occupied, so I went upstairs to call Luke. As far as I knew, he still had no idea what had happened and I wanted him to hear it from me.

Luckily, he answered the phone. "Hey, Luke, it's me."

"Hey, yourself. I was going to call you."

"You were?"

"My dad came home this morning. He still has a long road ahead of him, but at least he's home, in his own bed."

I let out a breath. "That's good. I bet he's happy to be with his family after everything he's been through."

Luke hesitated. "Some of them, I guess."

I frowned at the tension in his voice. "What do you mean by that?"

"Nothing."

"Come on, Luke. Tell me."

He took a breath. "It's just that I've been running this place since Dad went into the hospital. I've worked hard and have done a good job, yet the minute he gets home, he calls my two older brothers into his office. When I tried to join them he said they had ranch business to discuss and suggested I go see if Mom needed help in the kitchen."

I cringed. "Maybe he figured you needed a break because you'd been working so hard in his absence."

"Or," Luke countered, "maybe he still sees me as the youngest child who let him down by not following in his footsteps the way my brothers did. I know he's always been disappointed in me, but I thought my being here and handling things would help to change that. Now I'm starting to wonder if there's anything I can ever do that will get him to show me the same respect he shows my brothers."

"I'm so sorry."

Luke let out a groan. "No, I'm sorry. My father has been through a terrible ordeal and he has a terrible ordeal ahead of him. I shouldn't be making this about me. Maybe I really am the spoiled youngest child he thinks I am."

"Being the youngest is hard."

Luke's voice softened. "I know you understand. Are you at work?"

"No, I'm at my parents' house. Jason is in the hospital."

There was dead silence and then Luke spoke. "God, I'm sorry. Why didn't you stop me sooner?"

"I figured you needed to blow off some steam."

"What happened?"

I explained.

"Is there anything I can do?" I could sense the frustration in Luke's voice. It was the same thing I'd felt when his dad was in the hospital and I couldn't be there to help.

"No," I answered. "I think things are under control for now. Alana and the kids, as well as all my brothers, are staying at the house. Mom's baking with the kids, Alana is at the hospital with Jason, my dad is working in his office, and my brothers are trying to track down whoever did this to our brother."

"They wouldn't let you help out," Luke said.

"No, they wouldn't. And yes, I'm frustrated. Although I think Dad is too. I overheard John telling him to let them handle things before he left to join the other brothers in town. Dad was a cop for over thirty years and now his sons expect him to sit on the sidelines even though it was *his son* who was shot while looking into a case that was his to begin with. I imagine he's no more likely to sit around doing nothing than I am."

"Maybe the two of you should team up," Luke suggested.

I paused and then smiled. "You know, I suggested that to Dad last night. He didn't say yes, but he didn't say no either. I think he was just putting me off to avoid an argument in the hospital, but now that my brothers have sidelined him as well, maybe he'll feel differently. I think I'll see if he's at all open to the idea."

"Do I need to remind you to be careful?"

"No, you don't. I know you worry about me when I nose around in murder cases and I promise I'll be careful."

"Are there any suspects at this point?"

I let out a long breath. "No. Based on what I've been told, no one knows why Jason was even in the alley where it appears he was shot. We all think he had a hunch he wanted to follow up on, but it seemed he didn't share it with anyone. Hopefully, he'll be able to fill in some of the blanks when he regains consciousness."

"Hang on."

I waited while Luke shouted to someone that he'd be right down.

"My sisters just showed up, so I guess I should go. I'll call you later," Luke promised. "If you get any news about Jason call me. If I don't answer leave a message."

"I will."

"I love you."

"I love you too."

I headed to the kitchen, where my mom, Kala, and Kale were making enough food to feed an army.

"I thought you were just making cookies."

"I have a houseful of people to feed," Mom said. "I figured I should get ahead of the game."

I noticed Mom looked almost happy. I was sure she was worried about Jason, but it had been a long time since she'd had all her chicks at home. Or at least almost all her chicks.

"Is Dad still in his office?" I asked as I snagged a piece of apple from the pile she was slicing for a pie.

"As far as I know. You might want to leave him alone. He's in a foul mood. I don't think he took kindly to your brothers leaving him behind."

I took another piece of apple and headed down the hall. Luke had a good idea about Dad and me working together. Now all I needed to do was convince him of it. I knocked once on the door and waited.

"Come in," Dad called.

I opened the door and stepped inside. "Do you have a minute?"

He motioned to the leather chair on the other side of his desk. "What can I do for you, sweetheart?"

I glanced at the file he'd been working on. "The Cramer case?"

Dad nodded. "I had a few ideas I wanted to follow up on."

"I overheard part of your conversation with John."

My dad's lips tightened, but he didn't respond.

"Just so you know, I think he was wrong to exclude you," I continued. "I know you're retired, but you have more years on the force than the J team combined. In my opinion, they're foolish not to take that into consideration."

Dad let out a long sigh. "I suppose I felt the same way when I was younger. I remember several arguments I had with Grandpa after he retired. He was my father and I loved him, but I didn't appreciate the fact that he continued to provide me with little tidbits of information he was sure would help me do my job for years after he left the force. Still, it doesn't feel quite right to me to be excluded from an investigation into the shooting of my own son. I may be retired, but I'm not senile, and I'm as physically fit as I ever was. When John counseled me to sit this one out I felt like an old man."

"I wouldn't take it personally. The J team are close. They always have been. If you get with them one on one it's great, but when they're all together it's hard to break through. Trust me, I know."

Dad looked at me. 'Yeah, I guess you do understand. I was so happy to finally have a daughter after five sons, but I can see that being the youngest and the only girl was hard on you. I'm sorry I didn't do more to try to smooth the way for you."

I shrugged. "That's okay. Having to try to fight my way into the closely knit group the brothers presented has made me tough. Which brings me to the real reason I'm bothering you. I know you have something to offer to the investigation. So do I. I think we should work together if the boys won't let us work with them."

Dad frowned. "I don't know. While I agree you've grown up into a strong, capable woman, you're still my little girl, and this case has already proven to be dangerous. Besides, you aren't a cop."

"I know I'm your little girl and I know I'm not a cop—yet—but I'm smart and determined. I feel like there's a reason, a higher reason, I was the one who found the body at the bottom of the bluff. It seems fate has determined I be involved. I want to do this. I'm going to do this. I think we'd make a good team if you'll give me a chance."

Dad still hadn't answered.

"If Jason was able to talk to us I think he'd want us to work together," I continued. "He told me just the other day that I had a good head on my shoulders and he was recommending me for the next class in the academy."

"He told me the same thing. He said you were bright and intuitive and had proved to him you had what it took to be a good cop."

In that instant, despite everything else that was going on, my heart was bursting with pride. Not only was Jason proud of me, but it seemed my dad was as well.

"I'm going to call the resort to take a leave of absence," I said. "Maybe a week. I think you know me well enough to be aware that whether we work as a team or not I'm going to figure this out. I'll do it alone if I have to, but I think we'll be stronger together."

"Okay," Dad said.

"Okay?"

"We can work together if you think you can follow a simple set of rules."

"Okay. Anything." I was so happy that my father finally saw me as a capable adult, not just his baby daughter, that I had to clasp my hands together to keep from applauding.

"First, I call the shots. All of them. You aren't to go off and do anything on your own without my knowledge and approval."

"Agreed."

"And we're going to keep a low profile. We'll work from the shadows, and any information we manage to get our hands on will come to us legally."

"Agreed again."

"Okay." Dad pushed the file he'd been looking at across the desk to me. "This is everything I was able to discover about Clifford Cramer's involvement in the deaths of his wife and Roxanne Bronwyn five years ago. I think the answer lies in these notes. I'm just not sure where. I suggest we begin by familiarizing ourselves with everything I knew back then."

I nodded, accepting a pad and pen so I could start taking notes.

Once I was ready, Dad began to speak. "I was on my way home from a stakeout on another case when a call came over the radio that a woman living in the Aloha Heights neighborhood had heard a gunshot coming from the house next door. When I arrived there I found a woman, Roxanne Bronwyn, dead on a bedroom floor. She'd been shot. I went outside to take a look around, and that's when I saw a man, later identified as Clifford Cramer, running from the grounds. I followed and managed to trap him on the bluff at Sunrise Beach. He seemed to panic when he realized there was no escape and jumped. As we both know, the rocks at the bottom of the bluff prevent a safe entry into the water even during high tide. I assumed the man had died as a result of his fall."

I had no idea if I should be writing anything down at that point, but I wanted my dad to see I was serious, so I jotted down Cramer's name.

"Two days later I came across a missing persons report for Anastasia Cramer," Dad continued "The Cramers lived two doors down from Roxanne Bronwyn. Mrs. Cramer's sister had reported her missing the day before the shooting at the Bronwyn house when she failed to show up for a family reunion. I suspected her disappearance could be related to the death of Roxanne Bronwyn, so I went over to the Cramer home to look around. At that time I hadn't yet identified the man on the bluff as Clifford Cramer. In fact, I had no idea who he was. It was only after I arrived at the Cramer home and saw a photo of him that I was able to put two and two together."

I jotted down both women's names.

"Now that I realized the missing person had been married to the man who'd jumped from the bluff I began a thorough investigation." Dad sat back in his chair. "I managed to find a trace of blood on the lanai. I had a sample tested and learned the blood matched that of the female homeowner. An interview with the neighbor who'd called in the sound of the gunshot revealed that Mr. Cramer and Ms. Bronwyn had been having an affair. I assumed Mrs. Cramer had found out her husband was sleeping with their neighbor, confronted him, and, in an ensuing struggle, she was killed. I also assumed that for whatever reason, Mr. Cramer killed Roxanne Bronwyn the next day and fled the scene before jumping to his death. Neither of the Cramers' bodies were ever found."

"Until Tuesday," I supplied.

"Exactly. The fact that both bodies had been frozen came as quite a shock. It made me wonder if Mr. Cramer was responsible for either death or if there was another party who killed both women and Mr. Cramer just happened to be in the wrong place at the wrong time when I witnessed him fleeing from the Bronwyn estate."

"If Cramer hadn't killed Roxanne Bronwyn, why did he run from you? And, more importantly, why did he jump to what he had to know would most likely be his death?"

"I don't know. What I suspect is that everything that happened back then—and everything that has happened in the past couple of days—is linked, including Jason being shot. I intend to find out who shot my son and bring them to justice, no matter what my sons think of my ability to do so."

"I'm totally in."

Dad smiled. "I'm meeting the guys for lunch." I knew my dad was referring to three other retired HPD officers he regularly hung out with. "You're welcome to join us if you'd like."

I wasn't sure I'd ever been out to lunch with just my dad. He understandably had more in common with my brothers than with me, so I suppose it wasn't surprising he spent more one-on-one time with them than he ever did with me. Not that I was complaining. Exactly. I'd enjoyed quite a few mother/daughter shopping trips when I lived at home, and Mom and I still grabbed lunch together from time to time even now that I was out on my own. But lunch with my dad? Priceless!

"I'd love to," I finally answered in as neutral a tone of voice as I could muster, even though what I really wanted to do was jump up, raise my arms in the air, and shout hallelujah.

"Great. Run and get your things. We need to be at Callahan's in thirty minutes."

Callahan's was a bar that, while technically open to the public, was generally the type of establishment where men in blue and their guests could meet in a relaxed atmosphere. I'd always wanted to go there but had never been invited. Somehow, today felt like a rite of passage for me.

My dad and his three friends still referred to one another by their last names even though they were all civilians now. Thomas, Woodson, and McCarthy had all been to my parents' house on many occasions, so while I hadn't seen them in a while, I knew them fairly well.

"You remember my daughter, Lani," Dad said when we approached the table where the men were already sitting.

"Of course; how you doing, sweetheart?" Woodson asked.

"Okay, considering."

"I'm so sorry about Jason," Thomas said to my dad. "How's he doing?"

"Still unconscious but stabilized," Dad answered as he pulled a chair over for me.

"Every cop knows it could happen, but when it does it's still a shock," McCarthy said, sympathy in his voice.

"The boy is strong, like his old man," Thomas said. "I'm sure he'll be fine."

"Let us know if there's anything we can do," Woodson offered.

"The reason I asked Lani to come to lunch with us today is because we've decided to team up to look in to the shooting and we could use your help," Dad informed the others.

"I'm not surprised you're planning to investigate, but I kind of thought you'd ask your sons to help out," McCarthy commented.

When I noticed Dad wince I wanted to kick McCarthy beneath the table, but I controlled myself.

"The boys are looking in to things from one angle, but Lani and I are taking a different approach," Dad explained.

"You sure about this?" Thomas asked.

Dad smiled at me. "I'm sure. Lani has a lot to offer. Now, would you like to help?"

All three nodded. We paused to order before we got into the strategy session. I chose a brisket sandwich that looked absolutely fantastic and Dad ordered a slice of pizza. He took a few minutes to catch everyone up. He explained where we'd found Mr. Cramer's body and his wife's arm, and that both bodies had been frozen for an unknown amount of time before ending up in the water. Then Dad reviewed the events of five years before. I could see the guys were hooked once the case was presented.

"So, where do we start?" McCarthy asked.

"What about the information you gathered five years ago?" I suggested to my dad. "The witness statements. Any physical evidence. I think if we have a clear picture of the case you were building back then we'll find a clear place to jump into the current investigation."

The others agreed that was a good idea and my dad took out the file he'd brought with him. He began with the first witness he spoke to.

"I first interviewed the woman who reported hearing the gunshot that killed Roxanne Bronwyn. Edwina Hatfield lived in the house between Bronwyn and the Cramers. While the homes in the community were built on large lots, resulting in a good degree of privacy, I still figured if there was something going on between the two households she would be the one most likely to know about it."

I wrote her name down on my list.

"Ms. Hatfield informed me that she wasn't surprised to hear there had been problems between Roxanne Bronwyn and the Cramers," Dad continued. "She said Bronwyn had a lot of men and seemed to have made a lifestyle out of partying. She tended to play her men against one another and, in Ms. Hatfield's opinion, one of them probably had had enough of her cheating and teasing and took matters into their own hands. Ms. Hatfield also told me that she wasn't surprised to find Clifford Cramer had been seen running from the scene. Apparently, he'd cheated on his wife with many different women during their marriage, and given his proximity to Ms. Bronwyn, it seemed only a matter of time until they hooked up. She didn't know why Cramer would kill either her or his wife, and she didn't believe Anastasia Cramer would care that her husband had been having an affair with their neighbor because the two seemed to have an understanding between them."

"So Clifford Cramer cheated on his wife all the time and it was Ms. Hatfield's opinion that his wife knew and didn't care?" I clarified.

"Exactly. Ms. Hatfield indicated that the Cramer marriage had more to do with money than love, and as long as he provided her with the lifestyle she craved, she didn't care who he slept with outside the marital bed."

"Now that's my kind of marriage," Thomas chuckled. I knew he was a playboy who'd never married or had children. He was well into his sixties now, but he still maintained his reputation for being a ladies' man.

"Problem is, you don't have any money," McCarthy countered. "I think to have a trophy wife who cares only for your money you need to have some."

"Might have been able to afford a trophy wife if you'd laid off the ponies," Woodson added.

"So if it's true the Cramers had an open marriage, perhaps the theory that Mrs. Cramer confronted her husband about his affair and he killed her during the struggle that occurred as a result is less than believable," I commented, attempting to get the conversation back on track.

"In retrospect, I can see my assumption may have been inaccurate," my dad admitted. "It was a theory that made sense despite what Ms. Hatfield said, but now that it appears both Mr. and Mrs. Cramer's bodies have been frozen for five years, I'm beginning to think the person who killed Mrs. Cramer and Ms. Bronwyn may have been someone else entirely. That's something we'll need to figure out as we work on this."

I couldn't quite suppress the grin that crossed my face as I jotted down a few more notes. I'd never thought I cared all that much about my dad's approval, but I was wrong. "Okay, who else did you talk to?" I asked before the guys could start bantering again.

"At the time of Ms. Bronwyn's death, the house on the other side of Ms. Hatfield's home was occupied by a man named Chester Black, who has since passed away. He was nearly deaf and hadn't heard the gunshot, but he did confirm what Ms. Hatfield reported about Ms. Bronwyn's partying and multitudes of men. Most of what he reported confirmed what others had told me, but he provided one piece of unique information: Ms. Bronwyn had been married at one point, and while her husband had moved out years before, he was fairly sure the couple had never divorced. As it turned out, Mr. Black was correct. When Roxanne Bronwyn died her entire estate, worth several million dollars, was left to her ex, Phillip Orson, who lived in California."

"Wow; even I would tie the knot for several million dollars," Thomas admitted.

"Like you could get someone worth several million dollars," Woodson countered. "Now, if I'd met the woman before she was murdered she may have been convinced to hang up her welcome sign once and for all."

I rolled my eyes. Woodson had been married four times that I knew of and hadn't been able to hang on to any of his wives. Why he thought a woman like Roxanne Bronwyn would want anything to do with the scrawniest cop I'd ever met was beyond me.

I sat forward just a bit and once again tried to get things back on track. "So, if it turns out Clifford Cramer didn't kill Ms. Bronwyn, do you think Orson might have?"

"Possibly," my dad answered. "He had an alibi and there was no evidence that would demonstrate he'd really been on the island at the time of Ms. Bronwyn's death. I was sure Cramer was guilty. Why else would he jump to his death? But if it turns out he wasn't responsible for Ms. Bronwyn's death, I think we should take a closer look at her husband's movements at the time of the shooting."

"Do you know where he is now?" I asked.

"Actually, he moved to the island and is living in the house he inherited from his wife." Dad tossed a file folder to the three men. "There are witness statements from ten other people in this file, though none seemed relevant at the time. I think we should read them over and come up with a short list of people to reinterview. As I said, Mr. Black has passed on, but Ms. Hatfield still lives in the same home, and it won't be too hard to determine the current location of any others we feel might provide the most relevant information."

"Maybe we should divide up the list of people to interview between us. It'll go faster," I suggested.

There was a murmur of agreement around the table. The five of us discussed the various names in the file and after a bit of back and forth we decided who would be worth talking to.

"Lani and I will talk to Edwina Hatfield, Phillip Orson, and Craig Newton," Dad announced. "The three of you can take Darlene Porter, Carrie Silverton, and Veronica Quinn."

"I'll take Veronica," Thomas offered. Quinn had been Anastasia Cramer's personal trainer and there was a photo of the tall, buxom blonde attached to the file.

"Okay." Dad nodded. "Who wants Carrie Silverton? She was Anastasia Cramer's hairdresser and still works at the salon over at the mall."

"Woodson can't take lead on that one, considering he's gone bald." McCarthy snickered. "I'll take that one."

"And finally," Dad said, "Darlene Porter was Clifford Cramer's masseuse.

Woodson raised his hand. "That has me written all over it."

"Okay. Can you all meet back here tomorrow?" Dad asked.

The Three Stooges, as I was beginning to think of them, agreed they could, and the conversation changed to golf. I tuned out, trying to process everything that had happened in the past twenty-four hours. Talk about a roller-coaster ride.

Chapter 6

Dad had called ahead, so Edwina Hatfield was waiting for us when we arrived. She led us through her gorgeous home out onto a shady lanai that overlooked her pool and garden. She had freshly squeezed lemonade and three frosty glasses waiting in the refrigerator of the outdoor kitchen. We accepted her offer of the beverage, which was delicious.

"Thank you for agreeing to speak with us," Dad started off.

"Of course. I always wondered whatever happened to Clifford and Anastasia. To think they've been in cold storage for the past five years; it's almost unimaginable."

"It did come as a bit of a surprise," Dad admitted. "The reason I'm here today is to ask a few questions to uncover anything I may have missed during my investigation five years ago. Given the new information available, it seems my conclusion then may have been faulty."

"Of course," Edwina answered. "I'm happy to tell you whatever I can, although I'm not sure I know anything more than I told you then."

"Sometimes the smallest detail can make a huge difference," I encouraged.

"What would you like to know?"

"On the night Roxanne Bronwyn was shot and killed you called 911 after hearing a gunshot coming from the house next door," Dad began.

"Yes, that's correct."

"What time was it that you heard the shot?" Dad asked.

"Late. After eleven. I remember thinking just before I heard the shot that I'd finish watching the news and go to bed."

"And prior to the shot: Did you see anyone coming or going from the property next door?"

Edwina tapped her index finger against her chin. "No, I don't think so. Of course, I wasn't looking for anyone. Roxanne had a lot of visitors. Mostly men. I didn't pay much attention when there was a car in the drive. In fact, once I went upstairs for the night I always closed my blinds."

"Other than the shot, did you hear any noise coming from the house?" Dad asked.

Edwina shook her head. "No. Roxanne liked to have parties, but on the night in question the house was quiet. There were lights on, so I knew someone was home, but I didn't see or hear anything that would indicate she had guests."

"When we spoke five years ago you mentioned Clifford Cramer was one of the men who visited Ms. Bronwyn on occasion."

Edwina nodded. "Yes, that's true. Roxanne had many lovers and everyone suspected Clifford was one of them, although I didn't know that for certain."

"If Clifford Cramer and Ms. Bronwyn were having an affair do you think his wife would have minded that her husband and her neighbor were seeing each other?" Dad asked.

"No, I don't think so."

"Can you elaborate?"

"It seemed to me that Anastasia had her own men to keep her warm at night. I thought the couple had an open relationship that seemed to suit them both."

"Do you know the name of any of the men Mrs. Cramer had relationships with?"

Edwina paused. "There were several men who seemed to come and go on a regular basis, but I like to keep to myself, so I never met any of them. Except for Antonio, of course."

"Antonio?"

"The pool boy."

"Are you saying Anastasia Cramer was having an affair with the person who cleaned her pool?" I asked. I'm not sure why I was so surprised. A rich woman sleeping with her pool boy was a cliché.

"Yes," Edwina confirmed. "He cleans all the pools in the area, but I'm pretty sure Anastasia was the only one to whom he provided additional services."

I almost choked on my lemonade. I couldn't believe the prim and proper woman sitting across from me had referred Anastasia Cramer sleeping with the pool boy as *additional services*.

"Are you all right, dear?" she asked.

"Sorry. I swallowed the wrong way."

Edwina turned her attention back to my father.

"Do you know Antonio's last name?" he asked.

"Gomez."

"And do you have any idea where I might find Mr. Gomez?"

"He's here cleaning my pool on Tuesdays."

Dad narrowed his gaze. "So, Mr. Gomez still works in the area?"

"He owns the company now, but essentially, yes."

"Would you have contact information for him?"

"Certainly. Wait right here and I'll fetch it."

After Edwina returned Dad spoke with her for a few more minutes before we returned to his car.

"Sorry about the choking thing," I apologized. "I was just so stunned when Ms. Hatfield made her comment."

My dad chuckled. "It was pretty funny."

"Yet you didn't even crack a smile."

"Years of practice."

"So, what now?" I asked.

"Let's head next door to see if Ms. Bronwyn's husband is in. I didn't call ahead because I had a feeling he might refuse to see us if he knew what we wanted. If he isn't home now we'll try again later."

The home Roxanne Bronwyn had once lived in and Phillip Orson now owned was similar in size to Edwina Hatfield's. Dad rang the bell and the two of us waited for someone to answer. The likelihood that Orson might not be on the premises was pretty good—from the file we'd learned he owned homes in three states—but it didn't hurt to take a chance.

Luckily for us, the man answered the door. "Can I help you?" he asked.

"My name is Keanu Pope and this is my daughter, Lani," Dad introduced us.

"Pope? Are you the police officer I spoke to on the phone when Roxanne was murdered?"

"I am," Dad confirmed. "We have some new information in the case so we're taking a second look. Do you mind if we ask you a few questions?"

He stepped aside. "Come on in. I don't know anything at all about what happened, but I'll help if I can."

We all sat down and Dad asked Phillip how he'd met Roxanne, when and where they'd married, and when they'd separated.

"I met Roxi in Vegas more than fifteen years ago," Phillip began. "She was losing a lot of money at blackjack, so I gave her some tips. One thing led to another and I ended up in her room. I still don't know exactly what happened, but three days later we woke up and realized we'd gotten hitched at one of those twenty-four-hour chapels. We had a good laugh, figuring it couldn't have been a legally binding ceremony. Turns out, it was. Roxi had returned to Hawaii by the time we realized we were married, so I came over here to try to make a go of it. I know that may seem odd to some people, but Roxi lived alone and wasn't involved with anyone, and I was between jobs and needed a place to stay. Anyway, it seemed like a good idea at the time. We had a fabulous summer together after which we realized settling down wasn't for either of us. I went back to the mainland and eventually ended up in LA and Roxi stayed here."

"And you never got divorced?" Dad asked.

"We talked about it from time to time, but we never got around to filing the paperwork. It wasn't like either of us was interested in getting hitched to anyone else. After she died I got a letter from her attorney letting me know I'd inherited her entire estate. I happened to once again be between jobs, so I moved here. Like I told you when we spoke then, I wasn't on the island at the time of the murder and have no idea who could have murdered her. Roxi was a wild one, but she was a good woman at heart."

"Can you remember the last time you spoke to her?" Dad asked.

"I guess it was a week or so before I was notified of her death. She called to tell me that she'd reconnected with a man we both knew from the summer we spent together here. Neither of us had stayed in touch with him, and she wanted my opinion on what, if anything, he might really be after."

My dad frowned. "What do you mean by that exactly?"

"Fritz—that was his name, Fritz Meyers—was a nice-enough guy and the three of us had a lot of fun together that summer, but Roxi and I both thought there was something off about him. When he showed back up in her life she called to ask what I thought of it."

"What do you mean by *off*?" Dad asked.

Phillip shrugged. "Fritz liked to party, same as Roxi and me, but he had a serious side to him. It almost seemed like he had a reason for hanging out with us that he wasn't willing to talk about. For a while Roxi thought he might be working a con of some sort to get money out of her. We watched him real careful, but the con never developed and eventually he moved on. We talked about it later and decided we'd imagining things that weren't there."

"And you stayed in contact with Ms. Bronwyn even after you returned to the mainland?" Dad clarified.

"Sure. We always got on just fine; it was the whole till-death-do-us-part portion of our relationship that didn't quite fit."

"You said Fritz Meyers reconnected with her just prior to her death. Can you give us more information about that?"

"Roxi ran into him in Honolulu. He asked about me and she told him that we'd split up. He said he was going to be on the island for a few weeks and suggested they have dinner. She said sure. The next thing she knew, Fritz showed up on her doorstep, saying there'd been a mix-up with his credit card and he was being kicked out of his hotel. His return flight wasn't for another week and he wondered if he could stay with her. She wasn't sure that was a good idea, so she gave him some money and checked him into a nearby motel. Once he was settled she called me and we talked about it. We agreed letting him stay at the house wouldn't be a good idea and Roxi decided to pay for his motel through the date of his return flight. I'm not sure what happened after that. I never spoke to her again."

"Why didn't you tell me about Fritz Meyers when we spoke five years ago?" Dad asked.

"You didn't ask about him. It seemed you might have thought I had something to do with Roxi's death, which I absolutely didn't. You asked for my alibi, I gave it, and got off the phone as quickly as I could. I've seen on TV how saying the wrong thing can lead to all sorts of trouble even if you're innocent."

Dad didn't respond to that. I think he was beginning to realize he may not have handled the investigation as well as he could have five years ago. He asked Phillip if he knew where Fritz Meyers was now and he had no idea. Dad thanked him for his time and we left.

Dad suggested we head home to check in on things. Part of me wanted to follow the next clue, but another wanted to find out how Jason was doing. When we arrived at the house, Mom told us Jason was awake. He was groggy and didn't remember what had happened, but Alana was at the hospital and had requested that my parents join her as soon as they were able.

The J team were still out, so when Mom and Dad left I set to work entertaining Kale and Kala. Mom had already made enough food to feed an army, so I took the kids and Sandy down to the beach until it was time to get cleaned up for dinner.

******

"Aunt Lani let me surf with her," Kala informed her mother, whose face faded from a rich brown to a pale ash.

"It was all very safe," I assured Alana. "Kala was on the board with me and we surfed in teeny, tiny waves that can hardly even be called that."

"Was she wearing a life vest?" Alana asked.

I cringed. "I was hanging on to her the entire time. I promise you, if she had fallen—and she didn't—I would have jumped in right after her."

"You're a water safety officer. I would think you'd know it isn't safe for children to be in the water without life vests," Alana scolded.

"Yes, Lani," Mom agreed. "We trusted you to be responsible when you were left to look out for your niece and nephew. I thought you knew better than that."

"Lani always has had a careless streak," Jeff commented with a gleam in his eye. "Remember when she ran off when the family went camping that summer?"

"I was five," I pointed out.

"I don't think running off is the point. I think the point is putting my child's life in danger." Poor Alana looked like she was going to cry. I felt bad about adding to her already huge burden.

"You're right. I'm sorry. I was careless and I never should have taken the kids in the water without the proper equipment. It won't happen again."

I could see Jimmy snickering out of the corner of my eye. If he made some snide remark about me being sent to my room as some sort of punishment I was going to dump the bowl of potato mac over his head.

"So, tell us about your visit with Jason this afternoon." John, who appeared to have taken pity on me, changed the subject.

"He's awake and the doctor seemed to think most of the danger has passed. He does still have a way to go, however. He can move his legs, which is good, but he has a tingling in both feet. I guess recovering from such a severe injury just takes time."

"Did he know who shot him?"

Dad shook his head. "He can't remember anything from the day of the shooting. In fact, he seemed surprised when I told him about you finding the remains of Clifford and Anastasia Cramer."

"He has amnesia?" I asked.

"He remembers all but the last few days. The doctor told us patients with severe trauma oftentimes suffer from short-term memory loss. It was his opinion that Jason's memory would return over time, but he said some people never do regain the memories they lost. We'll just have to wait and see."

I looked at Alana. "I'm so sorry you have to go through this, and I know you'll want to spend time at the hospital with Jason. I want you to know you can trust me with the kids. If we go to the beach again it will be life vests all around. I promise."

Alana didn't respond, which made me feel even worse. The last thing I wanted to do was to upset or worry her. I'd been surfing since I was four years old and it hadn't occurred to me that Kala and Kale, both excellent swimmers, would need to wear life vests with me right there in the water with them. I didn't remember wearing a life vest when I first learned to surf, but Mom always made sure one or more of my brothers were with me.

"I think the kids and I are going to decorate the house for Halloween tomorrow," Mom offered.

I could see Alana was relieved her children would be spending the day with their responsible grandmother rather than their irresponsible aunt.

"Now that Jason is out of the woods I really should get back to work," Jimmy said. "I'll plan to come back on my next days off. Hopefully, Jason will be home by then, or at least able to have visitors."

"I should get back as well," Jeff said. "I hate to leave Candy home alone for longer than I have to."

I was about to suggest that Jeff could have Candy come to Oahu, but then I remembered that my mother and Jeff's wife didn't get along at all.

"John?" Mom asked.

"I'm going to stay for a couple more days. Justin and I are working on some leads and I'd like to see them through."

Although my brothers made me crazy at times, I realized I was sad to see them go. I was sure Justin would return to his own home tonight and I supposed I should go home too, but I'd enjoyed the brief time the Popes had been together as a family. I could see Mom was disappointed that her chicks were leaving the nest so soon as well.

"I'm off tomorrow," I informed my dad. "I can come over before we go to lunch."

"Dad and Lani are having lunch?" John asked, suspicion in his voice.

"Lani is my child, the same as you, and you and I have had lunch on many occasions," Dad reminded John.

"I guess," he said, but his expression communicated that he wasn't entirely satisfied with Dad's explanation.

Alana excused herself to put the kids to bed; Jeff and Jimmy got on the phone to book flights home; Dad, John, and Justin headed into his den; I decided to pitch in and help Mom with the dishes.

"I really am sorry about the life-vest fiasco," I said as I began rinsing the dishes.

"I know you didn't intend to put the kids in any danger. And they're strong swimmers. But Alana is already at the end of her rope, so I think it's important that we be extra careful."

"Noted, and I agree."

"So, what exactly are you and your father up to?"

I hesitated. I had no idea whether Dad intended to keep our investigation from Mom. "Nothing, really. He found out Jason was going to recommend me for the next academy class and wanted to take me to lunch to celebrate." I frowned. "I wonder if Jason even remembers he was going to recommend me."

"If not you can remind him when he's feeling better, although I have to admit you going to the academy isn't something I've been hoping for."

I opened the dishwasher and began stacking dishes inside. "You know how much it means to me."

"I do. But you're my daughter and my youngest. I spend enough time worrying about the boys. It was nice not having to worry about you as well."

Dad and the boys tended to protect Mom, so I was fairly certain she had no idea the amount of trouble I'd managed to get myself into even without the responsibility of wearing a badge.

"I know being the wife of a cop was hard on you. And I know being the mother of five cops has been even harder. And after what happened to Jason, I'm sure your fear has been amplified. I wish I could tell you that I was content working at the resort for the rest of my life, but we both know my time there was never going to be more than temporary."

Mom squeezed my hand. "I know. And I want to be supportive. But you are and will always be my baby girl. I'm never going to stop worrying about you. Having said that, my worrying shouldn't be a reason for you not to follow your dreams. I want you to be happy and I'll support whatever life path you choose."

I hugged Mom. "Thanks. I promise to be extra careful and not to give you cause to worry if I can help it."

******

Initially, I went back to the condo after I left my parents', but Cam and Kekoa weren't there, so I grabbed some clean clothes and Sandy and headed over to Luke's. I knew his house would be unoccupied as well, but I figured I could start decorating, which would help to divert my attention from the million things my mind was trying to convince me I should be worried about. Brody was sitting by the pool with Duke and Dallas when we arrived, so I grabbed a beer and sat down with them.

"Looks like the dogs are happy to see one another," Brody commented.

"Yeah, I think Sandy got used to us spending a lot of time here. He missed the boys."

"Luke told me that you might be staying here at least part of the time."

I shrugged. "I came over tonight to get started on the decorating, but I haven't made up my mind about what I'm going to do beyond that. I took some extra days off after I found out that my brother Jason had been shot, so I don't have to be back at work until next Friday. I might stay here a night or two."

"How's Jason doing?"

"He's awake and can move his legs, which is good, but he's suffering from tingling in his feet as well as short-term memory loss. I haven't seen him yet, but my parents assure me he's on the mend and will be fine with time."

"They catch whoever shot him?"

I shook my head. "Not yet. Justin and the guys are working on it and my dad and I are following up on some leads, but so far nothing has popped. I just hope we can track down the person who did this before they fade into the woodwork."

"I hear ya." Brody held up his empty beer bottle. "Unlike you, I have to work tomorrow, so I'm going to see to the horses and then head in. If you're still here tomorrow when I get home from work I'll help you with the decorating."

"Thanks, Brody. I appreciate it."

He stood up, then turned back to me. "Oh, I wanted to let you know, I officially told Mitch I'm going to take leave until mid-December, so no one will need to give up hours or be laid off."

"So, Luke's definitely going to be gone until then?"

Brody nodded. "I spoke to him today and he said he worked it out with his dad to stay until he's on his feet again. According to what his doctor told Luke, he's looking at a minimum of a month's pretty intense therapy. Luke said he felt better about having me help for such a long period of time if he were paying me. I figured given the layoff situation it was just as well. My last day at the resort before my leave is Monday."

I forced a smile. "Good. I'm glad it all worked out, and I'm sure Makena is relieved to know her job is safe."

"'Night."

"Good night, Brody."

I felt a tear in the corner of my eye as I watched him walk away. If Luke was definitely staying in Texas until mid-December I wondered why he didn't call to fill me in. Perhaps he was afraid I'd start crying, which would make it more difficult for him. The last thing I wanted to do was make things harder on anyone in my life, but it seemed that had been exactly what I'd been doing. But no more, I decided. If Luke needed space I'd give him space, and if Alana needed her kids to be in life vests I'd be darn sure to put them in life vests.

"You guys want to go for a walk?" I asked the three dogs.

They all began jumping around, which I took to indicate consent. It was already dark, so I grabbed a flashlight and set out along the well-worn trail that led to the top of the bluff. The stars certainly were beautiful. A flash of light streaked across the sky just as I reached the top of the bluff. I closed my eyes and made a wish. I'm normally not one to get sappy and sentimental over myth and folklore, but in that moment I really did hope the star would carry my wish to Luke, and that he and I would be wishing on the same shooting star.

Chapter 7

Sunday, October 29

I managed to get a good portion of the decorating done before I needed to head over to my parents' to meet up with my dad. I could already tell the house was going to look awesome. I wished Luke could see it, but it looked like that wasn't going to be the case. I'd called and left a long, upbeat message for him that morning, letting him know I was staying at the house, the dogs and horses were all doing great, and we all loved and missed him but understood that his priority was elsewhere right now.

He called back while I was in the shower and said he was sorry we kept missing each other but that he'd call me at noon my time. I then had to call him back and leave yet another message, saying I would be having lunch with my dad and then we'd be following up on a few leads, so could he please call me after five my time. I knew that would be ten his time, which should work out because he ought to have completed his obligations for the day by then.

I greeted my mom and the kids, then headed to my dad's office. He was in the middle of making some notes and held up one finger until he was done.

"I'm a little early," I started off.

"Actually, that works out perfectly. I just got off the phone with Antonio Gomez, the pool guy Ms. Hatfield mentioned. He's agreed to answer any questions we have if we come to the house where he's working this morning. It's on the way."

"Great. Were you ever able to track down Fritz Meyers?"

Dad stood up, opened his desk drawer, and took out his car keys. "I gave his name to Justin. I have no reason to believe he's still on the island, and given the limited amount of information we have to go on, I doubt we'd find him without the department resources."

"It seems he might have had something to do with Roxanne Bronwyn's death, although I can't see how he would be involved in the Cramers'."

"If he was a con man, as Phillip Orson suggested, he might be. Maybe he was running a scam on multiple families in the neighborhood."

Dad had a point. I hadn't thought about it that way. "What about Craig Newton? I remember he was on our list."

"He was a friend and sometime business partner of Clifford Cramer's. These days he owns a development company. I called his office and set up an appointment for this afternoon. I figured we'd meet with Antonio, have lunch with the guys, and then head over to see Newton."

"It seems you have everything under control."

Dad glanced at me. "You seem surprised."

I smiled. "Not at all."

The home where Gomez was working that morning was a nice but not overly extravagant one. Dad had been instructed to head around to the back when we arrived. Upon entering the yard, my suspicion that, based on his name and job description, he would be both hot and Latin, was confirmed. If Antonio Gomez was providing services on the side I could see why the women who employed him were lining up to take advantage of that.

"You made it." Antonio smiled.

"Your instructions were very clear. This is my daughter, Lani," Dad said.

I almost fell into the pool when the shirtless man took my hand in his, turned it over, and kissed my palm. "I am honored to meet such an enchanting young woman."

"I'm happy as well." *Happy as well?* There was no doubt about it: the guy was good. I loved Luke, but suddenly, I found myself wishing I had a pool in need of cleaning.

"How can I help you?" Antonio asked.

"As I indicated on the phone, we had a few questions we hoped you could answer," Dad responded.

"I will do my best if you don't mind talking while I skim."

"I don't mind at all," Dad replied.

Antonio picked up his skimmer and returned to his work while Dad and I walked along behind him.

"How long have you been in the pool-cleaning business?" Dad asked.

"Eight years. I started working for my uncle when one of his employees quit, but I found the industry to be much more entertaining than I could have imagined and I have since bought him out."

"And did you work in the Aloha Heights neighborhood five years ago?"

"*Sí.*"

"Do you remember having a customer named Anastasia Cramer?"

"*Sí.* Ana was more than just a customer. She was a friend as well as a lover. It was a tragedy when she turned up missing."

"I hoped you might know something about her disappearance, considering you were a regular part of her life at the time."

Antonio paused and looked at my dad. "I wish I could help you to find out what happened to Ana, but I'm afraid I know very little."

Antonio turned back around before leaning over to fish a leaf from the pool, causing his jeans to ride low. I must have gasped because my dad shot me a funny look before he continued his questioning. "Sometimes a little is enough."

Antonio once again stopped what he was doing and turned toward my father. "Ana was worried during the final weeks we were together. She wouldn't say what was weighing on her mind, but I got the feeling her husband was in some sort of trouble and had pulled her into that trouble along with him. After she disappeared I heard he had killed her, although I never thought that was the case. Cliff was a weak man and Ana was a strong woman. If there was going to be any killing in the marriage it would more likely have been the other way around."

"Do you think either one had a motive to kill the other?" Dad asked.

Antonio put his hand to his chin. His dark brown eyes looked thoughtful as he considered the question. "I want to say no, but there was something. The couple were well matched. They both had affairs and neither cared, yet they seemed to share a deep affection. I won't go so far as to say they were wildly in love with each other, but they had a deep friendship. As I said, there seemed to be some sort of a problem at the time of Ana's disappearance, but no, I never believed Cliff was responsible for it."

"What about Roxanne Bronwyn?" Dad asked. "Do you believe Cramer could have killed her?"

"*Sí*," Antonio said without hesitation. "Roxanne was not at all as hot-blooded as my Ana. Personally, she left me cold, but Cliff seemed to be enamored with her. More than that, I think he was in love with her. The problem was, Roxanne was only in love with herself. She played with men like Cliff, but she never gave any of them her heart. When the mouse taunts the cat, the mouse should expect that eventually the cat will attack. While I don't know that Cliff killed Roxanne, I wouldn't be surprised to find out it was true."

"Is there anyone else you can think of who might be able to fill in some of the blanks in what was going on in Anastasia Cramer's life prior to her disappearance?" I asked.

"You should speak to Eric."

"Eric?" I asked.

"Her tennis instructor."

"Would this be a tennis instructor with benefits?" I asked.

"*Sí.* You will find Eric at the country club near the Cramer home." Antonio picked up his skimmer once again. "I should get back to work. I hope you find your answers. Ana will always hold a piece of my heart."

Dad thanked him for his time and we left.

"What did you think?" Dad asked as we got back into the car.

"I think I need to move into a house with a pool."

Dad raised a brow.

"I'm kidding, of course. But it didn't seem to me that Antonio was hiding anything. I don't think he's guilty of killing any of the three victims, nor do I think he knows who is, but he did make an interesting point about Cramer dragging his wife into his troubles. I wonder what sort of trouble that was."

"I'd like to find out myself. Right now we need to meet the guys. Maybe if we have time this afternoon we can look in to the Cramers' financial history. From what I've heard Clifford Cramer was loaded, but if there were problems with their finances I could see how that would create problems in the marriage."

"Do you have access to things like financial records?" I asked.

"No directly, but I know a guy who does. You can't be a cop for more than thirty years and not stack up a lot of valuable connections."

By the time we arrived at Callahan's our sleuthing partners were already waiting for us. Aside from the reason Dad and I were working together, I was having the time of my life. He'd always been a fine father while I was growing up, but I'd often felt he'd left the parenting of his only daughter to my mother. I'd always dreamed he'd one day see me as more than just a girl and want to spend time with me, but he never had. For the first time in my life I felt like he was seeing me as a person, not just a little princess who showed up at the end of a long line of strong and capable sons.

I sat down between my dad and Woodson and grabbed my menu, focusing my attention on it as I tried to block out the extremely racy joke Thomas was telling. I wanted to be one of the guys, so I couldn't react with disdain to this guy-type humor; despite feeling I was blushing from head to foot, I didn't say a word. The waitress came over, bringing the guy talk to an end. I tried a burger today and my dad had a salad, which surprised me. Mom was always nagging at him to eat more salads and less beef, and he was forever arguing that he'd rather die young than die hungry. Maybe he liked salads after all, or maybe he was afraid I'd tattle on him if he ordered pizza two days in a row.

"What do we know?" Dad asked after we'd ordered.

"Well, I want to go on record as saying Veronica Quinn is hot," Thomas began. "And when I say hot I don't mean summer-afternoon hot, I mean surface-of-the-sun hot."

"Is there a point to all this heat?" Dad asked.

"Yes, there is. Veronica was Anastasia Cramer's personal trainer for almost three years. During that period she met Mrs. Cramer at her home; apparently, the Cramers had a home gym. Veronica said her conversations with her were centered on training, diets, and the hunk the lady of the house was currently hooking up with."

"We have reason to believe the pool boy, Antonio Gomez, was the hunk during one or more of those months," Dad told them. "Did the personal trainer mention any other names?"

"She claimed there was some sort of client/trainer confidentiality, so she wasn't at liberty to provide specific information, though she did say that in the weeks before Mrs. Cramer turned up missing, there was discord between her and her husband. Veronica didn't know all the details, but apparently, Cramer had gotten himself into some sort of hot water and wanted his wife to use her sexual prowess to get him out of it. She told Veronica that while she was usually up for some fun and games, the man her husband wanted her to cuddle up with gave her the heebie-jeebies and she wasn't comfortable with the whole thing."

"Did Mrs. Cramer provide any information about the guy she was uncomfortable with?" I asked. "Nickname, description, residence, job?"

"All Veronica would say was that he had a lot of influence as well as a lot of money. I had a feeling she knew more but was afraid. Before I left she warned me to watch my back."

I hoped that when Dad and I spoke with Craig Newton that afternoon he'd be able to give us the name of this person Cramer had been doing business with.

"Okay, Woodson, you're up," Dad said.

"I spoke to Darlene Porter, who's a masseuse. She didn't have a single good thing to say about either Cramer. She said the only reason she continued to provide massages to the couple was because they gave her a huge tip each time, and she was just getting started and needed the money."

"Why didn't she like them?" I asked.

"She said they were demanding and verbally abusive. They even tried to get her involved in a threesome at some point, but she turned them down. When they called for their next appointment she told them they'd have to find someone else, at which point they both apologized and offered her a huge bonus to come back. From that point on they were still mean but no longer inappropriate."

"Did she seem to know about anything that was going on in the household or with the couple that could have led to them ending up in the deep freeze?" Dad asked.

"She said there was a man. She didn't get his name, but one day he arrived as she was leaving. Mrs. Cramer looked very unhappy and uncomfortable when he showed up on her doorstep. She told him her husband wasn't home and he said he wasn't there to see him. Darlene got a strange vibe, and even though she didn't like Mrs. Cramer at all, she almost didn't leave. But Mrs. Cramer said everything was fine, that she'd see her next week. Darlene never saw either of the Cramers again."

Dad's eyes got big as he sat forward. "Did she give a description?"

"Tall. At least six-five. He was thin as a rail and had dark eyes, short dark hair, large ears, and a gold tooth one off from the center on the right."

"Sounds pretty specific," I commented.

"He gave her the creeps, so he made an impression."

"Do you think she'd work with a sketch artist?" Dad asked.

"I asked her that, but she said no. She has an eight-year-old daughter to think about and the guy looked like the kind of person you don't want to get involved with in any way, shape, or form. I told her that we'd keep her name out of it, but she said she worked with the police once before, after witnessing a rape, and they kept pressuring her to do more and more. First, they wanted her to provide a description, then they wanted her to pick the guy out of a lineup. When she'd done that the DA began pressuring her to testify. She said she'd learned her lesson and swore never to become involved as a witness again. To be honest, I was surprised she told me as much as she did. I told her I was retired HPD right up front. She told me I reminded her of her grandfather."

Thomas laughed out loud at that.

"Kekoa is a really good artist," I commented. "Maybe we can ask Darlene if she'll provide a description to the two of us in the privacy of her own home. We aren't cops and we can promise her we won't bring her name into it."

"Have Gramps ask her," Thomas said. "Maybe he can soften her up with a peppermint. My granny used them to bribe me when I was a kid."

"Very funny," Woodson responded. "But I'd be happy to talk to her again on your behalf if Kekoa agrees to the plan."

"I'll call her as soon as we're done here."

"Okay. McCarthy, you're up," Dad said. "It looks as if you've had a trim since yesterday, so I'm going to assume you were able to speak to Carrie Silverton."

"I did, but she claimed not to know a thing. Mrs. Cramer came in twice a month for a touch-up on her roots and a blowout, but, unlike with most of her customers, the two never talked. She said Mrs. Cramer brought her phone and texted the entire time she was there, except when her head was in the shampoo bowl."

"Did you believe her?" Dad asked.

"I didn't get the feeling she way lying. I guess I can speak to some of the other hairdressers in the salon to see what they have to say about it."

"If we need to. For now, let's see if we can get the masseuse to talk to Kekoa. Several people have mentioned that Clifford Cramer was involved with a man who made his wife uneasy. It sounds like the man Darlene saw could be the one. Lani and I have a meeting with Craig Newton this afternoon. Hopefully, by this time tomorrow we'll know more than we do today."

"Should we meet again?" Thomas asked.

"I don't see why not," Dad agreed. "How about we meet for a beer at around four?"

All three men were available. It was sad that these once very busy men had nothing better to do than get together for lunch or a drink three days in a row. Retirement, it seemed, might not be all it was cracked up to be.

I called Kekoa, who was fine with working with Darlene if she agreed. Woodson called her and arranged for us and only us to meet her at her home at five that afternoon. That was the time I'd told Luke to call, which meant I'd need to leave another message, suggesting we talk tomorrow morning. This long-distance-relationship thing was for the birds.

Chapter 8

Craig Newton was a harried-looking man in his midforties who made it clear the moment we walked into his tenth-floor office in Honolulu that we had fifteen minutes to ask whatever questions we had and not a minute more. Although the day was hot and humid, Craig wore a long-sleeved white shirt with black dress pants. A black jacket that matched the pants hung on a hook near the door. Although he'd instructed Dad to meet him in his office, I hadn't expected him to be working on a Sunday.

"Thank you for agreeing to meet with us," Dad said, diving right in. "As I mentioned on the phone, the remains of both Clifford and Anastasia Cramer were found earlier in the week, which is why we're taking a second look at both cases."

"You interviewed me five years ago when Cliff jumped from the bluff. You suspected he'd killed Anastasia and died himself from the fall. Are you telling me that wasn't what happened?"

"Given new information, it appears there may have been more going on than we initially believed.

When I spoke to you back then you told me you and Mr. Cramer had been friends for a number of years as well as worked together on several occasions."

"That's correct."

"Were you working together at the time of the incident on the bluff?"

"No, we weren't. Cliff wanted me to partner with him on a project he'd gotten involved in, but I declined. My unwillingness to invest in that project put a strain on our relationship. It had been more than four months since I'd seen or even spoken to Cliff at the time of his leap into the ocean."

"What can you tell me about the project he wanted you to invest in?"

I watched as Mr. Newton glanced at his watch, as if to determine how much of our fifteen minutes we still had left. He must have been satisfied we had enough time because he said, "Cliff was a gambler. While it's true that to survive as a developer you need to possess at least a bit of a gambling spirit, he was careless at times. The last project Cliff pitched to me was a condominium on one of the privately owned islands in the area. He insisted his business partner, a man he introduced to me as Skip Sellers, had a contract with the owner of the island to develop the land. I looked at the plans, but they seemed incomplete. I was also unable to confirm the existence of the contract Cliff assured me he had. I had a bad feeling about things, so I told him I was going to pass. He wasn't happy with my decision and tried on several occasions to change my mind, but eventually, I guess he realized my mind was made up because he stopped coming around. I later heard that when he couldn't find an investor he borrowed the money from a hard money lender."

"Do you know who he borrowed the money from?" Dad asked.

"Not for certain, but given the amount of money he was trying to raise, I imagine he borrowed it from a man named Akiyama. He has a reputation for having a lot of money to lend. He also has a reputation for collecting on his loans one way or another."

"Akiyama sounds like a Japanese name. Is he of Japanese descent?" I asked.

"Interestingly enough, no. He's very much Caucasian. It's my understanding his mother married a wealthy Japanese businessman when he was a boy. At some point he must have taken his stepfather's name."

"Can you tell me what he looks like?" Dad asked, "Tall, thin, dark hair."

"Does he have a gold tooth?" I asked.

"Yes, he does. Do you know him?"

I shook my head. "Someone else we spoke to told us Anastasia Cramer had a visitor who was described as a tall, thin man with a gold tooth just before she disappeared."

Craig chuckled. "Figures Cliff would try to use Akiyama's perversions to buy himself some time if he wasn't able to pay off his loan as agreed."

"Do you think Akiyama could have kidnapped Mrs. Cramer if her husband promised him his wife's favors in exchange for leniency?" Dad asked.

Craig shrugged. "He might have if he knew Cliff didn't have the money he was owed and if Anastasia refused to make good on an offer put forth by her husband."

I glanced at Dad. He nodded. We needed to take a closer look at Akiyama.

After we left Newton's office Dad drove me back to his house to pick up my car. He was heading to the hospital to visit Jason and I needed to go to the condo to meet Kekoa before we went to see Darlene Porter. On the way Dad and I had listed several people we needed to take a closer look at: Akiyama for one, Skip Sellers for another, and, of course, Fritz Meyers. I still wasn't sure whether Roxanne Bronwyn's death was related to whatever had happened to the Cramers or if it was a really strange coincidence that she was shot and killed the same week the Cramers had turned up missing.

******

"Have you been able to talk to Jason yet?" Kekoa asked as we drove to the address provided by Darlene Porter.

"Not yet. So far, the only visitors allowed have been Alana and my parents, but Dad was going to get an update when he visited this afternoon to let me know."

"Have your brothers all left?"

"Jeff and Jimmy went home yesterday, but John's still staying at my parents'. I know he's working with Justin on a few ideas the two of them came up with."

"Any chance they'd share their ideas with you?"

I shook my head. "The fact that they're being secretive doesn't bother me. I've been excluded from their projects and schemes my entire life. But I think

Dad is really hurt that they've shut him out. And I'm not sure why they have. I know there was a discussion about Dad getting older, and that they didn't want to put him in a dangerous situation, but in my opinion that's total malarkey. Maybe they're just afraid Dad will take over and start bossing them around. I don't know for sure what's going on, but the unwillingness of the J team to include Dad has opened the door for me to work with him, and I'm having the best time."

Kekoa rolled the window down a crack before she responded. "I know you've always wished your dad spent time with you the way he did with your brothers and I'm glad you're finally getting your chance. And it seems like you work really well together. Maybe this experience will be just the beginning of your working together. Oh, it looks like you need to make a left in about a half mile."

I slowed down just a bit as I watched for the crossroad. I didn't respond to Kekoa's comment until I made the turn. "I'm not sure how Dad feels about our partnership, but I'd welcome the opportunity to work with him again. Of course, if things go as I hope I'll be selected for the next class at the academy and it won't be too long before I'm a member of the HPD. I guess then I'll have to give up my sleuthing on the side."

"And how are you going to feel about that?"

"What do you mean?"

"Once you're hired by HPD you'll have a job, but you won't be a detective. You may see some action on the street, but when the detective in charge shows up you'll be back on patrol and he'll take it from there. Are you going to be content with doing the job you're handed while others carry out the investigations? Even if you're stuck handing out speeding tickets while someone else solves the murder you might have stumbled on while out on patrol?"

I had to admit I hadn't looked at things in quite that way, but Kekoa was right. Once I was on the HPD my hands would be tied. They wouldn't take kindly to a street cop getting mixed up in ongoing investigations. Not that they were thrilled when I did it now, but I didn't work for them, so they couldn't fire me.

"I wonder how long it will take for me to make detective. I mean, that's what I really want to do."

"I don't know how things work," Kekoa said, "but it won't happen right away. I'm really happy it looks like you're finally getting the chance you've always dreamed of, but you need to go into it with your eyes open. You're headstrong and you like to do things your own way. Ignoring the orders you're given because you don't agree with them is never going to fly once you're officially a member of the HPD."

"You're making a good point I hadn't thought through. I guess I'll need to do that before I commit to the academy." I glanced at Kekoa. "Do you think the reason Jason said he'd recommend me for the next class is because he thought my being a cop was the only way to keep me out of his way?"

Kekoa chuckled. "I think it's a good possibility that controlling your tendency to conduct your own investigations was the real motive behind Jason's sudden support of your dream."

Now that I thought about it, Jason had as much as said exactly that when we spoke. I'd been so happy to hear the news that I hadn't stopped to think about the message behind his words.

"It's that yellow house on the right," Kekoa said.

I slowed down, pulled over, and parked on the street. Darlene Porter lived in a small home, but it was in a nice neighborhood and from the outside it looked as if she kept the place in immaculate condition. The yellow siding was trimmed in white and the yellow vine roses that climbed a trellis near the entry gave the house a welcoming feel. Kekoa picked up her sketchpad and I grabbed my notepad before we headed to the covered porch leading to the front door.

"You must be Lani and Kekoa," a pretty young woman with long dark hair and bright green eyes said after opening the door.

"We are," I confirmed. "Thank you for agreeing to see us."

"And neither of you are cops?"

"No, we aren't," I confirmed.

"And if I agree to help with the drawing that'll be the end of it? I don't want this visit to be followed up with one from anyone in uniform insisting I get involved."

"The only people who even know Kekoa and I are here are my father and his friends, and we all agreed that if you helped us with the sketch we'd provide it to HPD as coming from an anonymous source."

Darlene looked Kekoa and me up and down for at least a minute before she finally stepped aside and let us in. Her daughter must have been elsewhere because it appeared we were alone in the house. Darlene showed us to a kitchen table where Kekoa could work and then began to describe the man she saw in extremely good detail. I remembered she'd been through the process once before and apparently remembered the drill.

"Would you say his cheeks were thinner or fuller than what I have here?" Kekoa asked.

"Thinner. And the eyes were closer together." Darlene paused to looked at the drawing again. "The brows should be thicker and the nose a bit longer."

I watched as Kekoa made the corrections. "How about now?" she asked.

"The chin should be narrower and better defined and the eyes should be dark, almost black. Yeah, I think you have it now. That's the man I saw entering the Cramer home that day."

"And that was the last time you saw Anastasia Cramer?" I confirmed.

"Yes. I heard she was missing a couple of days later. And after that I heard it was believed Mr. Cramer killed her, then jumped to his death."

"Did Mrs. Cramer refer to this man in any way?" I asked. "A name or a nickname?"

Darlene shook her head. "No. When she answered the door she said Mr. Cramer wasn't home. The man said he was there to see her, not her husband. I could tell Mrs. Cramer was uncomfortable with him, but she let him in and showed me out, even though I hesitated a moment, trying to decide if something bad was going on. At the time, I convinced myself this guy was just one of her men. She had a lot. But when I heard she was missing, I felt bad and realized maybe I should have told someone what I'd seen. The thing is, I have a daughter to think about, and the man looked like the kind you shouldn't make angry."

When we left Darlene Porter's house I called my dad to let him know I had the drawing. He was still at the hospital, so I said I'd drop it by his house. I asked if Jason remembered who had shot him and he said he hadn't, but he was going to be moved out of ICU that evening and would be allowed to have visitors if I wanted to go by to see him in the morning.

"Do you want to grab some dinner after I drop off this drawing?" I asked Kekoa.

"I could eat. Cam's playing poker tonight, so I'm totally free. In fact, I was going to offer to come over to help you with the decorations for the party."

"I got a good start, but there's more to do," I said. "How about we pick up some takeout and head to Luke's? We can eat, then tackle the patio. He has colored lights for the pool and patio area he's strung from the pergola. I thought we could add to the theme and try for a spooky yet enchanted feel."

"Sounds good to me," Kekoa said. "Does it still sound as if he won't make it back in time to attend?"

"Unfortunately, at this point it isn't looking good. I understand why he needs to be in Texas, but I miss him. I just wish he could find a way to come home."

"I'm sure he's missing you too, but that doesn't make it any easier. How about we stop by the condo and I'll grab a bottle of wine to go with our takeout?"

"Sounds like the best suggestion I've heard all day."

Chapter 9

Monday, October 30

I woke the next morning with a groan. Although it had been Kekoa's idea to have wine with our takeout, she'd only had one tiny glass, leaving the rest for me to finish off. I should have known too much wine would give me a headache. I wasn't a huge drinker, so it didn't take much to go to my head.

I grabbed an aspirin and a shower and took the dogs out for a walk. It was a beautiful day, somewhat on the cool side, which I very much enjoyed at this time of the year. I didn't have enough energy for a long walk, so I sat down on a rock under a large shade tree and called Luke while the dogs romped in the pasture nearest the house.

"Hello," a woman answered.

I frowned and looked at my phone. Had I called the wrong number?

"Is anyone there?" she asked.

"I'm sorry. I think I may have the wrong number. I was looking for Luke Austin."

"This is Luke's phone," the woman informed me. "Luke's in the shower right now. Can I take a message?"

"Uh, no. That's fine. I'll just try him later."

"Okay. Y'all have a good day now."

I hung up, took a deep breath, and began conversing with myself.

"Okay, Lani, don't freak out. Yes, a woman answered Luke's phone, but he has a mother and two sisters. It was probably one of them."

"Yes, he does have a mother and two sisters, but you've met all three of them, and chances are if the woman who answered his phone were his mother or a sister they would have realized you were the caller and said something. Besides, she didn't sound at all like any of the women who came to the island two summers ago."

"Then perhaps it was the maid. The Austin family is well off. They probably have a maid."

I decided to go with that explanation, even though I didn't believe it for a minute. I knew Luke loved me and I had no reason to make myself crazy by doubting that, so I'd just forget about the call and think of something else. I unlocked my phone once more and called my dad.

"Hey, Dad. What time did you want to get together today?"

"I was just going to call you, Lani. There have been some new developments, but I don't want to discuss them on the phone. Mom and I are just heading out to visit Jason. Can you come by the house at around eleven?"

"Yeah. No problem. I'll see you then."

I clicked off my phone after looking at the time. It was only nine. Kekoa and I had finished the decorating the night before and if I sat around for two hours I'd make myself miserable wondering about the woman who'd answered Luke's phone, so I called the dogs to me and headed back to the house. It would take about twenty minutes to drive to my parents' from Luke's ranch and I still needed to feed and water the dogs, which left me about an hour of free time. Just enough time, I decided, to check out a hunch and pay another visit to Roxanne Bronwyn's husband, Phillip Orson. Thinking back over the conversation Dad and I'd had with him two days before, it had occurred to me there were questions—important questions—we hadn't gotten to but really needed to be asked.

As before, I didn't call ahead, and he was home and seemed willing to talk to me. In fact, he seemed a lot more relaxed now that it was just me interviewing him than he'd been when my dad was with me. I supposed I understood that if my dad had considered him a suspect at the time of Ms. Bronwyn's death.

"So how can I help you, sweetheart?" he asked when we were seated at a table near his pool.

I hated it when people I didn't know called me *sweetheart* but decided to let it go in the interest of gaining the man's cooperation. "I've thought about things a bit since we spoke the other day and realized I had some additional questions. I hope you don't mind."

"If that means I can spend the morning with a pretty young thing like you I'm happy to answer any questions you have."

"Good. I appreciate that." I tried to sit up straighter to look taller, but when you're five foot nothing it's hard to look tall no matter what you do. "I've been thinking about Fritz Meyers. The timing of his being on the island in relation to Ms. Bronwyn's death seems suspect to me."

"Yeah, it seemed suspect to me too after I thought on it a spell."

"You said Roxanne put him up in a room until his flight, which was scheduled for a week after he showed up on her doorstep. Do you know if he would have still been on the island at the time of her murder?"

Phillip twisted his mouth, seeming to consider the question. "I'm trying to think back. It was a long time ago, but yeah, maybe. I remember Roxi called me and told me she was going to put Fritz up in the Seafarer Motel out on the highway because she wasn't comfortable with him staying with her. I guess it was just about a week later that I got the call that she'd been shot."

"I can get the exact date she was murdered from my father, but to know for sure if it occurred before or after Mr. Meyers's flight we'd need to know when it was scheduled or what dates she reserved the room for. I don't suppose you kept her credit card receipts?"

"I have everything that was here when I inherited the house. The lawyer recommended I hang on to stuff for ten years."

"Do you think we could take a look at the paperwork from the time of the murder?"

"Sure. It's in her office. Follow me."

When Phillip said he hadn't touched a thing he meant it. The room was covered in a thick layer of dust. "It would seem the motel room would be on the statement Ms. Bronwyn's received after her death. Do you have paperwork from after her death?"

Phillip picked up a thick envelope and handed it to me. "Her attorney took care of paying off all her debts, and once that was done he brought this to me. I'm guessing you'll find what you're looking for in it."

Phillip was correct. I did find the credit card statement, which detailed expenditures from around the time of Roxanne Bronwyn's death. There was a charge for the Seafarer Motel for eight nights beginning on October 15. That meant Fritz Meyers must not have been scheduled to fly home until October 23. I texted Dad to ask him if he remembered off hand the date of the murder. He texted back October 21.

So, Meyers would most likely have been on the island.

"My father saw Clifford Cramer run from his property after he responded to the call about the gunshot. Because he not only fled when he was told to freeze, then jumped from the bluff, Dad assumed he was responsible for Ms. Bronwyn's death. He followed up with a few other leads, like his call to you, but I don't have the sense an intensive investigation was carried out."

"Based on what I've heard, it does seem Clifford was guilty." Phillip nodded.

"Maybe. But if he wasn't that means someone else was there. I wonder if any of the neighbors might have seen something. Edwina Hatfield has already said she didn't see anything, and I know the neighbor on the other side has passed away, but what about the neighbors across the street? Do you happen to know if any of them lived here back then?"

"Sure. Nosy Nellie has lived directly across the street since back in the day when I spent the summer here with Roxi."

"Nosy Nellie?"

"Old gal. Can't hear a thing, but she still seems to know everything that's going on with everyone. She has herself a set of powerful binoculars and she sits up there in her attic at the top of the house and spies on everyone."

"So if someone else was here she may have seen them?"

Phillip nodded. "Yeah, I guess she might have at that. Word of warning, though, if you plan to head over to talk to her. Nellie is meaner than a cougar with a splinter in his paw. You best be careful if you don't want to get mauled."

"I'll keep that in mind." I started to stand up. "Before I go I have one more question. What did Fritz Meyers look like?"

"Tall. Skinny. Big eyes in a little head."

"Was his hair dark or light?"

"The guy was as bald as a cue ball."

"Okay, thanks. I appreciate you taking the time to answer my questions."

"Anytime, little lady. If you have anything else I can help you with you come on back. I appreciate the company."

I said good-bye and left. I didn't have reason to believe Phillip was lying to me, but something felt off. I just couldn't put my finger on exactly what it was.

I still had a little bit of time before I needed to meet my father, so I decided to see if Nellie was home. I wasn't sure how I was going to converse with a woman who was deaf because I didn't know sign language, but I figured if she was home and willing to speak to me I'd cross that bridge when I got to it.

My first hurdle, I realized when I arrived at the woman's front door, was how to announce my arrival. I supposed she might have a service dog or a flashing light attached to her doorbell, so I knocked and rang the bell too. I waited a full minute, then repeated the process. I figured if the bell was attached to a flashing light she might not see it right off. I was debating the idea of ringing the bell for the third time when the door flew open.

"What do you want?"

I froze. Should I respond? Did the woman read lips? She'd asked, so I decided to verbalize my request. "Hi. My name is Lani. I was hoping to speak to you about Roxanne Bronwyn."

"She's dead."

Okay, so she either wasn't totally deaf or she read lips.

I continued. "Yes, I'm aware of that. I hoped you might have seen something on the night she was shot that would help us figure out who did it."

Nellie narrowed her gaze but didn't answer right away. It looked like she was sizing me up, so I stood perfectly still and tried not to squirm.

"Didn't see anything." She tried to shut the door.

"Wait." I put my hand on the door to hold it open. I turned to look over my shoulder at the house across the street where the murder had occurred. "I realize you don't know me, but I really would appreciate just a few minutes of your time."

I turned back to the woman, who was staring at me with a blank look on her face. "I need to look at you when I speak, don't I?"

She nodded.

Of course; I should have realized. "I'd really appreciate just five minutes of your time. I'm trying to figure out who killed your neighbor. I can tell you're an intelligent woman who knows a lot more than she lets on. So, how about it? Five minutes?"

"Five minutes," she responded. Instead of inviting me in, she stepped out onto her porch. I guess I couldn't blame her.

I spoke clearly and slowly so I wouldn't lose her. "On the night that Roxanne Bronwyn was shot a man ran from the grounds. The police officer who responded chased him."

"Clifford," she stated.

"Yes. That's right. Did you see him run away from the police officer?"

Nellie nodded.

"Do you think he shot Roxanne?"

Nellie shrugged.

"Can you elaborate?"

"The two were sleeping together; Clifford was at the house often. As far as I can tell, he seemed to really care about her. I saw him arrive at the property on many occasions with flowers or a gift. I can't see why a man who cared about a woman enough to bring her flowers would kill her, and I didn't see him enter the house the night Roxanne died."

"But you did see him flee?"

"Yes, I did. It seemed he might have just arrived via the fence at the back of the property he often used to sneak in at night when the cop saw him and he ran."

"But you didn't actually see him enter the grounds through the back gate?" I clarified.

"No, I didn't. I suppose it may be possible he was already at the house before I started watching."

"You speak remarkably well for someone who's deaf."

"I haven't always been deaf. It happened slowly, over time, and I learned to read lips to compensate for not hearing everything people said. And I remember how to speak. Is that really what you want to discuss with the three minutes you have left?"

"No. I'm sorry. So, you saw Clifford running from the officer who responded to the shooting, although you didn't see him actually enter or exit the house."

"Isn't that what I just said?"

"Yes. It is. Did you see anyone other than Clifford enter the house that night?"

"Just the cop."

"Okay, then did you see anyone other than the cop leave the house?"

"Nope. Not until the next day."

"Who left the next day?"

"Why, Clifford, of course."

Chapter 10

If Nellie was correct about what she saw, it proved Clifford Cramer hadn't died the night he leaped into the water. I did have to wonder, however, why he returned to Roxanne Bronwyn's house after the police left. I needed to get going if I wanted to make it to my parents' by eleven, so I headed in that direction. Dad had said he had news. Maybe whatever it was combined with what I'd just learned would provide us with a better idea of exactly what had happened five years ago.

As soon as I arrived, he invited me into his office and asked me to sit down.

"How's Jason doing?" I asked.

"Better. He seemed more alert today and said the tingling in his feet is all but gone. They're even talking about letting him go home in a couple days as long as his vitals remain strong."

I smiled. "That's wonderful news. Did he remember who shot him?"

Dad shook his head. "He's regained part of his memory leading up to the incident but still doesn't remember who shot him. He did say he'd been following up on a hunch that the plastic bags you found in the water had at one time contained bricks of cocaine."

I thought back to those bags. While I hadn't retrieved them, they'd appeared to be empty. I supposed whoever dumped Cramer and his frozen wife into the sea could have dumped the drugs as well. But why?

"So, if the bags did contain drugs are we thinking the Cramers were involved in some sort of a drug deal?" I finally asked.

"I'm not sure. I spoke to Justin before I went to see Jason. He said he tracked down Fritz Meyers, who admitted he'd been on the island the week before Ms. Bronwyn's death, trying to create a situation where she'd agree to take him in. Once he realized she wasn't going to do that he changed the date for his outgoing flight and was back in Las Vegas when she was shot. Justin checked with the airline and confirmed he had indeed left the island prior to the murder, as he claimed."

"So we can eliminate him as a suspect."

"Unless he flew home and then returned to the island immediately after, I think we can. Justin said he didn't think he had a motive to want Roxanne Bronwyn dead. He admitted to having a thing for her and wanting her to invite him into her life, but that was it. Meyers told Justin he stopped by her house on several occasions before he finally decided to leave, and on one of those occasions Cramer was there. The two of them were arguing about something she had that he wanted. He wasn't sure what it was, but according to what Meyers told Justin, Cramer was pretty intense about retrieving property he believed to be his."

I sat back to let things roll around in my mind. It seemed they were finally falling into place. "What if Clifford Cramer was looking for the drugs?" I asked. "I stopped by to speak to the neighbor directly across from the house where Roxanne Bronwyn was shot. Apparently, she likes to spy on her neighbors through binoculars. She told me that she saw him coming out of the home the morning after the shooting."

"So he didn't die in the fall?"

"Apparently not," I confirmed.

Dad steepled his fingers. "So, here's what we know, or at least what we've been told and suspect to be true. We've been told Clifford Cramer was involved in some sort of business transaction with a man named Skip Sellers. He was unable to convince his friend and sometimes business partner Craig Newton to invest with him, so he had to borrow from a hard money lender who we assume was Akiyama. When Cramer couldn't meet his repayment deadline, he offered him the services of his very attractive wife to buy more time. A masseuse who worked for the Cramers saw a man arrive at the Cramer home looking for the wife when she was leaving. We suspect it was Akiyama coming to collect the favor Cramer had promised him. The fact that Mrs. Cramer was never seen again until her arm showed up in the water last week indicates to me that the man must have taken her to another location."

"Okay, so Akiyama kidnaps Anastasia Cramer and then tells her husband he'll only release her when he's repaid the money he's owed," I jumped in. "Cramer has a plan to get the money, but he needs something that's at Roxanne Bronwyn's home to do it. Maybe drugs, maybe something else. She won't give it to him; they struggle and he shoots her, either intentionally or accidentally. He sees you arrive, freaks out, and flees. Later, he jumps into the sea and somehow survives. He may have been familiar with the area and known exactly where to jump. He returns to Bronwyn's home the following day to get whatever it was he was after, which is when the neighbor saw him coming out of the house."

My dad took over at this point. "Cramer either sells what he took from Ms. Bronwyn's home or maybe whatever he took was what Akiyama was after all along. He tries to barter it for his wife's release, but instead of letting her go he kills Cramer too and puts both of them on ice."

I frowned. "I like the theory so far, but why put the Cramers on ice? Why not just dump them in the sea or bury them in some remote location?"

"That part does seem odd," Dad admitted.

"And why dump them all these years later?" I added.

Dad didn't answer right away. On one hand it felt like we were narrowing in on something that made sense, but on the other there were still way too many loose ends to allow us to pat ourselves on the back. Plus, the theory we'd come up with didn't explain who'd shot Jason or dumped the Cramers' bodies in the sea as recently as last week. Akiyama? If he did kill the Cramers it made no sense for him to dump them now. And what was up with the plastic bags? If Cramer had tried to use the cocaine to barter for his wife why would whoever killed them dump the drugs, or at least the plastic bags they'd been stored in, into the ocean?

"Okay, what about this?" I began again. "We've been told Akiyama is a hard money lender. We suspect Cramer borrowed from him, then tried to use his wife to buy himself more time. We also suspect Cramer needed something Roxanne Bronwyn had hidden in her home to use to barter for his wife's release. If Akiyama did kill the Cramers I suppose it would make sense that he would store the bodies on a property he owned. What if he recently sold the property and needed to dispose of the bodies, so he snuck them onto a boat and dumped them in the ocean? I guess one could argue that whatever was in the plastic bags could be used against him, so he disposed of that as well."

"We still have a theory without proof of any sort," Dad said. "We need more."

Dad was right. We needed either an eyewitness or conclusive physical evidence.

"What about the freezer?" I asked. "If Akiyama killed the Cramers and stuck the bodies in a freezer on his property, and if he sold that property, prompting him to finally dispose of the bodies, maybe we can narrow down the property. He may have disposed of the bodies but still have the freezer. If we can find that we should be able to find DNA evidence linking Akiyama with the Cramers."

Dad grinned. "Good thinking, Lani. Very good thinking indeed."

I can't begin to explain how good his words made me feel.

"I'm going to call a friend who should be able to get me information regarding property owned by

Akiyama five years ago and anything he's recently sold. Maybe we can find a location," he said. "Once we have that we'll go take a look. If we can find the freezer the Cramers were kept in all these years we might really have something. In the meantime, I'm going to call Justin to see if we can verify that the man the masseuse saw was indeed the one we suspect had come to collect a debt."

"Okay. I'll say hello to Mom and the kids while you do it. I think I saw them out by the pool. Just holler when you're ready."

I was happy to see Kala and Kale were relaxed and having a good time, but I wondered why they weren't in school. It was, after all, a Monday. I sat down next to my mother, who was watching the kids from the shade and asked that question.

"Alana is going to take them home when she gets back from the hospital," Mom explained. "It's time for them to get back to their normal life now that Jason's doing better. The kids didn't want to go to school until they felt better about their father, so Alana agreed to keep them out of school today so they could get settled back in their own home."

"I guess that makes sense. I heard Jason might be able to go home this week."

"Yes," Mom answered. "He's doing much better. I overheard the doctor speaking to Alana about releasing him as early as Wednesday or Thursday."

I squeezed Mom's hand. "That's great news. I was pretty scared there for a while."

"We all were, but Jason is strong. I knew he'd pull through."

"It was kind of nice having all the other brothers here all at once," I said.

"It's been a long time," Mom said. "I spoke to them about coming home for Christmas. John said he'd planned to come anyway and Jimmy said he'd already asked for the time off. It's our year to have Jason, Alana, and the kids, and Justin said he'd try to work out his shifts to be here for dinner. Which just leaves Jeff. He said he'd talk to Candy about it, but we both know she isn't likely to want to spend the holiday with me."

"You could apologize," I said. Mom had made it very clear she'd thought Jeff had made a huge mistake when he married Candy, and the two women had been at odds ever since.

"Yes, perhaps it's time. I thought she'd break his heart by this point, but they seem to be making it work." Mom turned and looked directly at me. "How about you and Luke? Can I count on you as well?"

"You can count on me, but I don't know what Luke's plans are. I guess you know he's still in Texas."

"Your father filled me in. How's his father doing?"

"Better, but he still has a way to go. Luke's committed to staying until his dad can go back to work, which seems unlikely to be for quite some time." I let out a long breath. "I'm not sure if Luke even plans to come back. I can imagine a scenario where he decides to stay in Texas."

Mom put her arm around me. "I know how hard this must be for you, but I'm certain things will work out the way God intends."

"Yeah, I guess." I wanted out of this conversation very badly. "I need to make a phone call. If Dad comes out tell him I ran to my car but will be right back."

When I got there I dialed Luke's number and prayed he'd pick up. I'd been desperately trying not to let the idea of a woman answering his phone while he was in the shower ruin my whole day, but despite my best efforts, the jealousy kept sneaking through.

When I got Luke's voice mail I almost broke down in tears, but instead I took a deep breath and left a message. "Hey, Luke, it's me. I just wanted to let you know that Jason is doing better. He should be able to go home later in the week. I hope your dad is continuing to improve as well. Dad and I are going to follow up on a lead when he gets off the phone, so I'll probably have my ringer off. We're meeting with the guys at four my time, so maybe you can call me at three my time? If that doesn't work just text me a time that does and we'll find a way to make it work out." I paused as a tear escaped from the corner of my eye. I wasn't sure what else to say, so I simply hung up.

I returned to the patio, where Dad and Mom were talking. "Do you have news?" I asked.

He nodded. "I'll fill you in on the way." Dad kissed Mom on the cheek, then placed a hand on my back and led me toward the garage.

As soon as we were on the road he began to fill me in. "I was able to confirm that the man in the drawing Kekoa made from Ms. Porter's description is the one who goes by the name Akiyama. That's his surname, which he got from his stepfather. His first name is Bryan. Apparently, he hates it and never uses it."

"So, if it was Akiyama who came to the house on the day Mrs. Cramer went missing, then our theory works, at least so far."

"Yes, at this point," Dad confirmed. "My friend was able to provide the information I requested. Akiyama owned three properties five years ago, all of which have recently changed hands. I have the addresses, so we can check them out. If we can find the freezer we may have something."

"Don't you think Akiyama would get rid of the freezer as well as the bodies?" I asked.

"It depends. If both bodies were placed in one freezer it would need to be fairly large. If he believed the bodies wouldn't be recovered, he'd have no reason to suspect we'd be taking a second look at the case and there wouldn't feel any pressure to get rid of the freezer."

"Yeah, but once we found Cramer's body and his wife's arm don't you think he would?"

"Perhaps. But it won't hurt to take a look. The first property is a single-family home. In my mind, it's the least likely to have housed the freezer, but it's on the way to the two more likely ones."

"How long has it been vacant?"

"My source didn't know. He just knew Akiyama owned it back then and sold it a month ago. Like I said, it's the least likely to provide what we're looking for, but it makes sense to follow all leads. If there's one thing I learned after more than thirty years as a cop it's that oftentimes the answers you seek are found in the most unlikely places."

Chapter 11

The first property was a single-family house in a quiet neighborhood. All the homes were older ones on large lots that backed the forest. Each had a detached garage that most residents used for storage rather than an automobile. The yard here had been unattended for quite some time, which made it appear the house had been vacant prior to being sold.

Dad and I tried both the front and back doors, which were locked. We looked through the windows, which didn't reveal much other than outdated carpet and dingy walls in need of paint. We headed to the garage, which opened onto a dirt drive. Fresh tire tracks were clearly visible on the hard-packed dirt, which seemed to indicate that while the house may have been unoccupied someone had visited the garage fairly recently.

"Can I help you?" a man who looked to be around seventy asked us.

Dad held out a hand in greeting. "Keanu Pope. I'm interested in buying this house and hoped to take a look around. I wasn't aware it was vacant."

"Been empty for a lot of years," the man said. "At least the house has been empty. The previous owner used the garage as a storage room. If you're looking to buy the place I'm sorry to say you're too late. A van showed up last week and took everything that had been stored in the garage. One of the moving men told me the house had been sold."

Dad appeared to be disappointed. "That's too bad. The place needs work, but it seemed perfect for my daughter."

"Guess you can check with the new owner. They might be willing to sell it for a profit."

"I might just do that," Dad said. "Do you mind if we take a look in the garage? My daughter is an artist and was interested in turning it into a studio."

"Sure. I hope things work out of you. It'd be nice to have some younger people living in the area."

The man returned to his home and Dad and I headed to the garage. Fortunately, the door was unlocked. We entered the large space to find it empty. There were multiple footprints and the dirt pattern on the floor indicated there had been items arranged in rows with walkways between them.

"What do you think was in here?" I asked.

"I don't know." Dad knelt and looked at the cement. 'If Akiyama used this space for storage it could just have been things relating to his business."

"He's supposed to be a hard money lender; it doesn't seem lending people money would require storage."

"He owns businesses and properties in addition to lending money. I'm sure owning property for income could lead to a certain amount of repair work, which would require tools and replacement parts. What I don't understand is why he left this house sitting empty. He could have rented it for a lot more money than it would cost him to rent a room in a storage facility."

"Maybe whatever he had stored here was illegal and he wanted to stay under the radar," I suggested.

"I guess that would make sense." Dad stood up and walked across the room. "There's an overhead light, but I don't see any wall plugs, so unless he ran an extension cord to the freezer, it most likely wasn't stored here. Let's head on down the road to the second property, which I think has a lot more potential to be what we're looking for."

We got back into the car and drove toward the highway heading west.

"My phone is about dead. Do you have a charger?" I asked.

"In the glove box."

I plugged in my phone, then settled in for the ride. It was a gorgeous day and I may as well sit back and enjoy it. Fretting over Luke being away wasn't going to bring him home any sooner and I was enjoying the time I was spending with my dad.

The second property was a warehouse, which seemed to me a good place to keep a freezer full of bodies. It was close to the marina. If Akiyama had transported the bodies to a boat that would have made for a relatively short trip between it and the freezer.

The building wasn't much more than a large metal shed standing on a large, fairly isolated piece of property at the end of a narrow dirt road. Dad's car was new, so he took it slow once we hit the unpaved portion. The metal building was tall and windowless, and except for the absence of bay doors, it reminded me of an airplane hangar. I didn't know if this had been the location used to store the Cramers' remains, but it seemed like as good a place as any.

There was a small door at the side of the building that, thankfully, was unlocked. We entered it to find it completely empty except for a large garage-style freezer with a top-opening lid sitting against one wall. Industrial size and grade, it seemed obvious it would take a crane to move it, which was probably why Akiyama had left it behind when he sold the property. The freezer was unplugged and empty, but there was a slight trace of blood in the seam at the bottom.

"Bingo," Dad said. "Let's call Justin and tell him what we found."

"Not so fast," I heard a man say from behind us.

I turned around to see a large man with dark hair pointing a gun at us.

"We were just leaving," I said, taking a small step forward. The man shot at my feet, causing me to jump back. I watched in horror as Dad reached behind him for the gun he kept in his belt, only to have the man shoot him in the leg before he could bring his arm back around. I screamed as Dad fell to the floor.

"You shot him," I accused him.

"He was going for a gun. He left me little choice." The man grabbed a couple of short ropes that had been on the floor near the freezer. "You." He pointed the gun at me. "Tie up the old man."

I hesitated, and the man pointed the gun to my head.

"Just do it," Dad said.

I did as the man asked.

"Now the gun," he instructed. "Take it carefully from his waist and set it on the floor."

Again, I did as he said.

"Now kick it toward me." He had the gun pointed at Dad's head now. "No funny stuff or the old man dies."

I did as he demanded.

"Now empty his pockets."

I took Dad's wallet, car keys, and cell phone out of his pants pocket and set them on the floor. The man took a step forward and picked up everything, including the gun. "Now you: empty your pockets."

"I don't have anything." I held up my hands in a show of surrender. All I wore was a tight tank top and a pair of short denims; it was easy to see I wasn't lying.

"Okay, then, sit down with your back against the wall."

I did as he said.

"I'd shoot you right now, but the boss might want to have a word with you first, so I'll just lock you in. Don't worry; you won't have long to wait. As soon as Truman called, the boss sent me over here because I was closer, but he's finishing his meeting before he'll be on his way."

With that, the man left the building, closing the door behind him. I heard him lock the door from the outside and then drive away.

I knelt next to my dad and untied his hands. When he was free I tore his pant leg. "We need to stop the bleeding." There was a small hole where the bullet had entered that hadn't appeared to damage any bone, but the wound was bleeding quite a lot. I pulled off my top and applied pressure to the wound. "I need you to apply as much pressure as you can to your leg while I try to figure out a way out of here."

Dad put his hand over my now-bloody top. "Unless you can find a way to get the door open there doesn't appear to be a way out."

I tried the door, which was constructed of heavy metal and was locked. I stood in my bra and shorts and looked around the room. Except for the freezer, the room was empty. There were narrow air vents at the top of the building along the roofline. They were small, but so was I, so I thought if I could make my way up the flat metal wall I could squeeze through. The vents had to be a good twenty feet off the ground, however, and, sadly, I wasn't Spider-Man.

"I'm going to try to get up to those vents," I informed my father.

He looked up to where I was pointing. "How?"

The freezer was about four feet high, which would help but wasn't nearly enough. There was a rope hanging from one of the rafters, but it was at least eight feet off the floor, so there was no way I could reach it. If I climbed up on the freezer it would give me the height I needed to reach the rope, but it wouldn't be close enough to the freezer to simply reach out my hand, so I'd have to make a leap of faith, hoping I could grab the rope before I fell to the floor.

I turned and looked at my dad. "Okay, here's the plan. I'm going to climb up on the freezer and then leap across to that rope overhead. I'm going to see if I can reach one of those vents."

"There's no way you're going to get to that rope from the top of the freezer."

"I have to try."

"I don't want you getting hurt."

"If I can't figure out a way to get us out of here I have a feeling getting hurt is going to be the least of our problems."

By the look of resignation on his face, I could see Dad agreed I needed to do something. "Say you do get hold of the rope. Then what? Even if you make it to the rope and climb to the top how are you going to reach the window?"

I kicked off my flip-flops. "How about we take it one step at a time? I'll hurry. Just don't die."

"I won't. Please be careful."

"I will."

I climbed up onto the top of the freezer in my bare feet. The rope was close enough to make it possible to reach but not enough to make it *easy* to reach. I took a deep breath and shoved off with my legs as hard as I could. I grabbed on tight when I felt the rope between my hands. I slid down just a bit before tightening my grasp, which left me with a painful rope burn I'd need to tend to later. For now, I had to climb. I wrapped my legs around the rope and started up one hand over the other until I reached the top.

When I got to the top of the rope I considered what to do next. The air vents had screens on them, and other than a very narrow ledge I thought I could grab on to, there was nowhere to get a foothold. I also needed to reach the wall with the vent, which was several feet away. I grabbed onto the rope with my hands, then unwound my legs. I kicked back and forth as hard as I could, which set me swinging. When the rope swung far enough for my feet to reach the wall, I kicked at the screen with them. Luckily, it popped out and fell to the ground on the other side of the wall. I kicked again, directing my right foot and leg toward the opening. When it went through I bent my knee, then let go of the rope with my hands. I almost fell on my head to the hard floor below, but I was able to grab on to the small ledge with one hand at the very last moment.

I heard my dad gasp as I paused to catch my breath.

"Are you okay?" he asked.

"I'm fine. Once I get through the vent I'll drop to the ground and try to get help."

"It's a pretty long drop."

"Don't worry. Falling out of the window is the easiest part of my plan."

It took some work, but somehow, I managed to get both my legs out of the window with my stomach resting on the ledge. The top part of my body was still inside the building and I didn't have room to turn to look at the ground below, so I had to hope I'd land on something soft after I finished squeezing myself through the narrow opening. The ledge scraped my stomach and chest as I crammed myself through. At one point I was afraid I was going to get stuck half in and half out, but I didn't give up, and eventually, I was hanging by my hands on the outside of the building.

I glanced down at the hard dirt below. At least there weren't any large rocks, but I suspected a fall from this height was going to hurt quite a lot. I really didn't have a choice, though, so I hoped for the best and let go. I tried to land feet first, but one leg hit the ground before the other and I fell to my side, reaching out with my arm as I did so.

Damn.

I was pretty sure I had broken my wrist, but I couldn't worry about that just then. I'd also twisted an ankle, but somehow, I managed to hobble to Dad's car. It was locked, so I found a rock to break a window, grabbed my phone, and called 911. I felt sure everything would be fine as long as help arrived before the boss—who I suspected was Akiyama—arrived to finish what his thug had started.

Chapter 12

When I saw the dust from a vehicle on the dirt road I began to panic until I saw it clearly enough to realize it was a patrol car. I didn't recognize the cop who first responded, but after I explained what had happened, he ushered me into the car, then headed to the building to get my dad. By time he got the door open, two additional patrol cars as well as an ambulance had showed up. Dad and I were both whisked into the ambulance before I could ask to speak to Justin, but I could fill him in on everything we'd learned after I made sure Dad was going to be okay.

As it turned out, my wrist was fractured but didn't require surgery. They took a few X-rays, then applied a removable cast. My ankle was sprained but not broken, so they wrapped it in a bandage, treated my rope burns, and fixed up all my scrapes and scratches. After I was as cleaned up as they could make me, they released me. I headed over to the nurses station to find out where they'd taken my dad just as Justin rushed in through the door.

"I was just coming to find you." Justin wrapped me in a hug.

I held up my arm. "Ouch."

He took a step back. "Sorry."

"It's okay. How's Dad?"

"He's in surgery, but I think he'll be fine. I know you're worried about him, but time is of the essence right now. I need you to come down to the station with me."

I must have hesitated because Justin put a hand on my cheek and looked me in the eye. "Alana is with Mom and Kekoa went to stay with the kids. You can do the most good by helping me nail the guy who did this to Dad."

I looked down at the hospital gown they'd given me to wear because I didn't have a top on when I was brought it. It wasn't fancy, but it would have to do. "Okay, let's go."

When we arrived at the police station Justin had someone find me some clothes. Then he took me into a room where a detective was waiting. Justin was a street cop, but he'd been allowed to help with the case because it was his brother, and now his father, who had been shot.

I was given a moment to change into the baggy T-shirt one of the female cops brought and then we settled down for the questioning.

I started off by sharing the theory Dad and I had come up with. "As you know, five years ago my dad responded to a call that led to his discovery of Roxanne Bronwyn, a gunshot victim. He saw a man, later identified as Clifford Cramer, run from the scene and gave chase. Cramer leaped into the ocean from the bluff at Sunrise Beach. It was assumed he'd died in the fall and had been carried out to sea. It was later discovered his wife was missing. It was assumed Cramer first killed and disposed of his wife, then killed Ms. Bronwyn, who he was reportedly having an affair with, before jumping to his own death. That theory held until last week, when I found Cramer's body at the bottom of the bluff at Sunrise Beach, as well as the arm of Anastasia Cramer floating in the water neat Dolphin Bay Resort. That led to my brother Jason taking a second look at the Cramer case. He was shot and nearly died for his efforts."

I paused to take a breath while Justin and the detective sat and waited. After a few seconds I continued.

"After Jason was shot my father and I decided to conduct our own investigation. After all, my father was the cop who initially responded to and handled the case five years ago. He had the background knowledge and insight my brothers," I looked directly at Justin, "decided not to utilize."

Justin flinched.

"After it was discovered that both Cramers had been frozen prior to being placed in the water last week my dad and I began looking at things from a slightly different perspective," I said. "During our investigation we found some interesting things that led us to our theory."

I took a sip of the water I'd been given.

"It seems Clifford Cramer entered into a business relationship with a man named Skip Sellers. He also tried to bring his friend and occasional business associate Craig Newton in on the deal. When Mr. Newton refused to become involved, Mr. Cramer appears to have borrowed from a hard money lender,

Akiyama. We suspect that when Cramer couldn't meet his repayment deadline, he offered Akiyama the services of his very attractive wife to buy more time. But it seems Mrs. Cramer, while sexually liberal, was uncomfortable with Akiyama, who seemed unwilling to take no for an answer. A witness saw a man meeting his description arrive at the Cramer home looking for her. The fact that Mrs. Cramer was never seen again until her arm showed up in the water seems to indicate he must have kidnapped her."

I paused to take another sip of water. Neither Justin nor the detective had said a word since I'd begun to speak. "My father and I believe Cramer had a plan to get the money he needed to buy his wife's freedom, but he needed something that was at the home of his mistress, Roxanne Bronwyn. We believe whatever he was after was stored in the plastic bags I saw near Cramer's body. It could have been drugs or something else. We also believe Ms. Bronwyn refused to give Cramer what he wanted, they struggled, and she was shot. When he saw my father he ran, which led to him jumping into the water and somehow surviving. We also have a report from a neighbor who saw Cramer leaving the Bronwyn home on the day after she was shot and killed, so we assume he returned to the house to get whatever it was he was after."

I took another deep breath. "My dad and I believed that once Cramer was able to obtain what he was after he went to Akiyama and tried to barter for his wife's freedom. It was at that point we suspected both Cramers were killed and their bodies put into a freezer. We never did figure out why they were frozen rather than simply buried or dumped in the ocean, but we felt finding the freezer would give us the link between Akiyama and the murders. We figured if we could provide that link we could ask HPD to open an official investigation into Akiyama's involvement in the murders.

"So Dad called in a favor and found out which properties Akiyama had recently sold and then the two of you went off half-cocked and got Dad shot," Justin finally said.

"Dad and I were on our own because you and the brothers refused to work with us even though we had insights to share," I countered. "I feel awful about Dad being shot, but that was as much your fault as mine, so don't try to pin it all on me."

The detective smiled, but I could see he was trying to hide it. "Please continue, Ms. Pope," he said after sending a stern glance Justin's way.

"My father and I thought the timing of the bodies showing up in the ocean after all this time was relevant and we suspected Akiyama finally disposed of them because he sold the property where they had been stored. We identified the properties he'd owned five years ago and had recently sold and came up with a list of three. The first property was a single-family home. We spoke to..." I paused. "Damn. The old man must have been working for Akiyama. That has to be how the thug knew what we were doing."

Justin and the detective glanced at each other.

"We spoke to a neighbor at the first property," I explained. "He seemed like a nice old man, but I'm just realizing he must have ratted us out."

"Please go on with your story," the detective encouraged me.

"There isn't a lot more to tell. Almost as soon as we arrived at the second property the thug snuck up on us. He shot Dad, then locked us in the building. I climbed up a rope and slipped out an air vent, then called 911. The rest you know."

A woman came into the room and whispered into the detective's ear. He smiled. "We have the man we believe shot your father in custody. Would you be willing to pick him out of a lineup?"

"Damn right I would."

Once I'd identified the dirty, rotten lowlife who shot my dad, he was arrested and led to an interrogation room. The detective who'd interviewed me planned to also interview him. I was told to go home and he'd call me if he had any additional questions. Justin offered to drive me home, which was a good thing; I was exhausted and didn't want to wait for another ride.

I was still irritated with Justin for his comment about Dad and me going off half-cocked, so it was a chilly ride until he finally said, "I'm sorry."

I turned and looked at him.

"I should never have suggested Dad getting shot was in any way your fault," he added. "If anyone is to blame it's me. I knew Jason had shared some information with you lately, which was something I was very much against. But it should have occurred to me that if our older brother trusted your instincts enough to work with you, and our father trusted your instincts enough to make you his partner, maybe I should have as well. Do you forgive me?"

I smiled. "I forgive you. I know you and the other brothers still see me as your little sister who needs to be protected, but I've grown up. I've worked hard and

I have skills to offer the team. I honestly don't believe any of you could have leaped from a freezer to a rope, climbed it, squeezed through an air vent, and saved the day."

"That may be true, but it's equally likely that none of us would have ended up trapped in the warehouse in the first place."

I hated to admit it, but Justin was probably correct. I did have a special knack for ending up in dangerous situations. "Will you call me to let me know how things work out after you interview the man who shot Dad?"

Justin hesitated for just a second before agreeing to do it. After he dropped me at the condo I realized my car was still at my parents', so I ended up calling Cam and asking him if he could take me there to retrieve it when he got off work. After I hung up with him, I called Callahan's and asked the bar's owner to let Thomas, Woodson, and McCarthy know we wouldn't be meeting them for drinks after all.

Chapter 13

Tuesday, October 31

"Do you think we have enough ice?" I asked Kekoa as we prepared for the Halloween party.

"Yeah, we have plenty. I'm wondering if we should have bought more chips, though. You know everyone gets the munchies when they drink."

"We have enough food to feed half the people on the island. We're fine. Hand me that bag with the cups and plates and I'll set them out."

Kekoa handed me the bag and I began to arrange the items on the table despite the bulky cast on my arm. Everything looked awesome. I found I was actually excited about the party that only yesterday had seemed like just a huge distraction.

"So, you were going to tell me what happened with the guy who shot your dad when Cam called and interrupted us," Kekoa urged.

I stopped what I was doing and turned my attention back to her. "So get this: The guy has been working for Akiyama for ten years. In that time he's done a lot of pretty bad things, but he'd never killed anyone. My brother convinced him to talk in exchange for some sort of immunity deal he worked out with the district attorney. The guy spent the next six hours spilling his guts about Akiyama and all the people he's swindled and killed or had killed."

"So?" Kekoa asked, with just a slight tone of impatience in her voice. "What did he say? Did he provide the missing pieces to the puzzle you've been working on?"

"Pretty much. Basically, Dad and I were spot-on with our theory. Clifford Cramer did get into a business deal with Skip Sellers that he couldn't follow through with once his friend refused to go in with him. He did borrow money from Akiyama, which he was unable to pay back on time, so he did offer his wife's services in exchange for additional time. The wife did balk at the idea, so Akiyama kidnapped her and made her comply forcefully. Cramer showed up with a bunch of cocaine he hoped would pay off his debt. The problem was, while Akiyama was a money lender who had both swindled and killed many people, he drew the line at selling drugs."

"You're kidding!"

"Nope; it's true. Anyway, when Cramer showed up with the coke Akiyama killed both him and his wife and put their bodies in the freezer."

"Why did he do that?"

"I don't know for certain, but by the time Cramer approached Akiyama the police already knew Roxanne Bronwyn had been shot and Mrs. Cramer was missing. Maybe he figured there was too much heat, so he'd freeze the bodies and dispose of them later."

"I guess that makes sense. And it does make sense he could have forgotten about the bodies until he sold the warehouse and needed to clean things up." Kekoa paused as she set up salami and cheese on a tray. "Do we have more wine?"

I began to slice the fruit for the sangria. "In the pantry."

"So how does Jason being shot fit in to all this?"

"That's the really strange part. It doesn't."

"Come again?"

"Jason finally remembered what happened. It seems once he found out about the plastic bags he suspected cocaine was involved, so he went to confront a dealer he knows in the area. One of the dealer's men shot Jason when he showed up demanding to see his boss. It turned out Jason being shot had nothing to do with the Cramer case at all, other than that it was Roxanne Bronwyn's coke that got Jason to confront the dealer in the first place."

Kekoa began mixing the dip. "That's pretty random. I guess the only thing I don't understand now is why the bags from the coke were in the water."

"Akiyama dumped the coke when he dumped the bodies. He must have a strong reason for his dislike of drugs, although I don't know what it is. I'm not sure why he hung on to the coke for five years before getting rid of it; perhaps he stashed it with the bodies and forgot all about it."

"Okay, final question: If Cramer didn't die on the rocks the night he jumped into the ocean why did the watch he was wearing when he was found stop at midnight?"

I shrugged. "I have no idea. He could have broken it in the jump. Of course it makes no sense he would have kept it on if it was broken, unless it had some sentimental value. That's one mystery that probably will never be solved."

"I'm just glad the case is wrapped up and all the Popes managed to survive. The past week has been terrifying for me; I can't imagine what your poor mother went through."

"Yeah, it's tough being the one who stays behind and keeps the home fires burning while her husband and children go out every day risking their lives. I think this experience had given me a new appreciation for how she provides the glue that keeps us all together."

"It's nice you got out of this closer to her."

"It is. I'm going to take her to lunch later in the week to thank her for all she does." I looked at my phone for perhaps the fifth time since Kekoa and I had been working together.

"Are you expecting a call?" she asked.

"Luke. We missed each other all day yesterday. With everything that was going on it was mostly my fault, but I've called him five times today and every time it goes directly to voice mail. He must have his phone turned off."

Kekoa raised a brow. "That seems odd."

"And there's more. When I called him yesterday morning a woman answered his phone. She said he was in the shower and offered to take a message."

"Maybe it was one of his sisters or his mother."

"I've met them. It wasn't."

Kekoa crossed her arms in front of her. "Surely you don't think Luke is cheating on you?"

"I don't want to think that, but the longer it goes without a return call the more insistent my mind is that cheating is exactly what's going on. What am I going to do?"

"You're going to put that silly thought out of your head and enjoy the party you've worked so hard on. I'm sure there's a reasonable explanation why Luke hasn't called you today and once you speak to him you'll see it."

I sighed. "Yeah. I guess. I'm heading out to the porch to get the tubs for the beer."

Kekoa and I worked side by side for another hour. Things were really coming together, but we still needed Cam to help with the setup of the fog machine.

"Where's that boyfriend of yours?" I asked. "Shouldn't he be here by now?"

Kekoa stopped what she was doing and glanced at the clock. "He should be here. Hang on. I'll get my phone and text him."

"Wait, I see his car," I said as he pulled off the main road and onto Luke's private drive. I watched as Cam, dressed as a surfer, which was pretty much the way he always dressed, got out of the driver's side door, while a giant gorilla got out of the passenger side. "Who's that?"

"I don't know, but he has to be cooking in that heavy costume."

Cam came into the house first, grabbed Kekoa by the hand, and headed out to the patio. I watched as the ape entered the kitchen. I was about to ask who he was when suddenly I knew. "Luke?"

He pulled off his giant ape head. "How'd you know?"

I didn't answer but instead ran across the room despite my sprained ankle, jumped into his arms despite my broken wrist, wrapped my arms around his neck and my legs around his waist, and gave him the kiss I'd been dreaming of for more than a month.

******

Later that evening, I lay in Luke's arms totally satiated and totally content. It had been a spectacular party and I'd enjoyed getting together with all my friends, but the first guests had arrived shortly after Luke and Cam, so for most of the evening I'd found myself wishing they'd all go home.

"Are you home to stay?" I finally asked the question that had been on my mind all night but had been afraid of hearing the answer to.

"Just for a week. I probably shouldn't have come now, but I woke up in the middle of the night missing you so much that I called my older brother and asked him to cover at home, found a crappy but expensive flight, bought a last-minute ticket, and headed west."

My head was on Luke's chest as he held me in his arms. I couldn't see his face, which was just as well because I was glad he couldn't see my disappointment when he'd said he was going back.

"It's been hard having you gone, but I totally understand," I said when I was sure my voice wouldn't crack with emotion.

"Part of me wants to just tell my family I have my own life—a life I love—and need to get back to it, and part of me is happy that for the first time my family needs something from me. That's the thing about being the youngest. Everyone takes care of you and watches out for you, but no one really expects or needs anything from you."

"Boy do I get that," I said. "While I'm very sorry Jason was shot and incredibly sorry the family had to go through it, for the first time in my entire life I think my father finally saw me as a capable adult. Like you said, my brothers and parents have always treated me like some fragile princess, but now that I saved my father's life, I think they can finally see I have something to offer."

"So we'll just do what we need to do," Luke said.

Uh-oh; there was the sadness again. "We will. We'll Skype and try to be better about connecting. And then, when your dad is back on his feet, you'll come home and we'll make up for lost time."

"I'd like you to continue to stay in the house. If you want to." Luke rolled over so I was on my back and he was looking down at me. "In fact, if you want to, I'd like you to stay."

"Forever?"

"Exactly. I know I won't be here at first, but I should be home in another month or six weeks. In the meantime, I can take comfort in the idea that you're here in my bed waiting for me."

"You want us to live together?" I clarified.

"I do. You can use the time I'm away to redecorate. I want you to feel like this is your home too. So how about it? Will you share my life?"

I wanted to say yes, but I found myself begin to panic.

"And just so you know," Luke added, "I want us to get married. Someday, when you're ready. I told you I wouldn't bring it up until you were ready, but I want you to know that marrying you and having a family with you is my endgame. I just figured living together was a good first step. So, will you be my roomie?"

I fought the urge to flee and instead pulled Luke's head down to mine. "Yes," I whispered in the last fraction of a second before his lips met mine.

Chapter 14

Wednesday, November 8

My heart was heavy after dropping Luke off at the airport that morning, but there was hope as well. During the past week he'd helped me move all my stuff into his house—I mean, *our* house. He'd taken me shopping for a few new things like towels and dishes we picked out together, and then set me up with a bank account I could draw from to complete the redecorating we'd started while he was away. We promised to make each other a priority and never go to bed without having talked that day, and he promised he'd be home well before Christmas, one way or another.

Dad had called and asked me to stop by the house on my way home, which was where I was headed now. Both he and Jason were home from the hospital and doing well. It had been a really hectic couple of weeks, but it seemed things were falling into more of a regular pattern.

"Dad here?" I asked my mom after letting myself in the front door.

"In his office. He's expecting you."

I headed down the hall, knocked once, and then entered the room after Dad told me to come in. He got up from his chair, came around his desk, kissed me on the cheek, and held the chair for me until I sat down. All the extra attention was beginning to make me nervous.

"Is anything wrong?" I asked.

"Not at all," Dad said as he sat back down in his chair behind the desk. "In fact, things are better than they've been in a long time."

"You're looking better," I said.

"The leg hurts at times, but I'm on the mend, and I'm sure I'll be back to my old self soon. I asked you here today to discuss a couple of things with you."

And back to nervous. "Okay," I said. "What's on your mind?"

"First, I want to thank you for saving my life."

I started to say it was nothing, but Dad didn't give me the chance.

"Not only did you keep your head in a crisis but what you did to escape the warehouse was truly amazing. I can honestly say that all five of your brothers working together couldn't have done what you did that day."

Uh-oh. Here came the tears.

"Working with you has finally made me see what you've been telling me all along. You're an exceptional young woman with a lot to offer. The HPD would be lucky to have you. However," Dad glanced at my arm, which was still wrapped in a cast, "I'm afraid you'll miss the next academy class. I know how much you were looking forward to it and feel bad you're going to miss your shot because of me. But I have a proposal I hope you'll consider."

"A proposal?"

"Working with you brought home how bored I've been since I retired. I love your mother and we agreed I'd retire while I was young enough to travel, but I feel like I still have a lot to give, and we don't share many common activities. I've given this a lot of thought and I've talked it over with your mother and come to a decision."

"You're going back to work?"

"Yes and no. I'm going to open a detective agency."

Wow. I hadn't seen that coming.

"The skill set I've acquired can be extrapolated. I have my pension, so I don't need to make a lot of money. If I have my own business I can work on the cases that interest me and turn down those that don't. And I can make my own hours and plan time off to travel if Mom gets the bug."

"That's wonderful, Dad. I'm so happy for you. It sounds perfect."

"It does, doesn't it? The only thing that would make it better would be if I had a partner I know I can trust and depend on. Someone like you."

I was so stunned I couldn't speak.

"I know your dream is to be a cop like your brothers. And if that works out at some point, I'd let you out of your obligation. But in the meantime, would you be my partner?"

"Yes, yes, yes." I hopped up out of my chair. "I'd love to work with you. More than anything else in the world."

Later that evening I looked back on the past few weeks and realized Lani Pope was about to begin a new chapter in her life.

Up Next From Kathi Daley Books

Preview Book

Monday, December 11

"Fifty-three years ago, Francine Kettleman—
Frannie K for short—lived at the Turtle Cove Resort
while her husband, Tom, was away in Vietnam.
Frannie, who was just nineteen when she arrived on
Gull Island, lived there from April 1963 to August
1964. During her stay, Frannie received love letters
from a man named Paul, who was also stationed in
Vietnam. Years later, the letters, which Frannie had
tied together with a ribbon, placed in a metal box, and
hidden in the wall of the cabin where she was living,

were found by the contractor in charge of the remodel of the resort. After a cursory investigation, we know that on August 14, 1964, Frannie was found dead in a cemetery fifty miles from here. It's believed by most that Frannie was the fourth victim of the Silk Stocking Strangler, a mass murderer who was never caught or identified. The Strangler was credited with killing thirteen women over a ten-month period from 1964 to 1965. All the victims were strangled with a pair of women's silk stockings, and all were found in cemeteries along the East Coast from Florida to Massachusetts."

I paused to look around the room at the people who had gathered to hear my proposal. I could see this case had everyone's attention. Love, intrigue, and tragedy all wrapped up in one package. We'd stumbled upon the letters Frannie had left behind before Thanksgiving, so we were familiar with the specifics, but in the interest of tradition, it was the task of the submitting author, who in this case is me, Jillian Hanford, to officially present the case to the other members of the Mystery Mastermind Group.

"Are you asking us to track down a serial killer?" Alex Cole, a fun and flirty millennial who made his first million writing science fiction when he was just twenty-two, asked.

I turned to answer him. "Not at all. If Frannie was indeed killed by the Strangler, finding her killer is beyond our ability to research."

"Is there any doubt Frannie was a victim of this madman?" Brit Baxter, a blond-haired pixie and aspiring writer of chick lit, asked.

"While I haven't yet come up with any hard evidence that would indicate Frannie wasn't the fourth victim of the Silk Stocking Strangler, I do have reason to question that assumption. I recently met with Ned Colton, who was the deputy in charge on Gull Island when Frannie was murdered. Given the fact that her body was found fifty miles away, and the FBI was already investigating the Silk Stocking Strangler, Ned wasn't asked to take an active part in this investigation. Ned shared with me that he took the liberty of looking in to things on his own. He admitted that, on the surface, it appeared Frannie *had* been murdered by the Strangler, but there were some anomalies he found interesting."

"Anomalies?" Victoria Vance, a romance author who lives the life she writes about in her steamy novels and my best friend, asked.

"The Silk Stocking Strangler had a signature of sorts. He always abducted his women at night, he used silk hosiery to strangle his victims, and he always chose women who were blond, blue-eyed, and between the ages of twenty and twenty-four. He always left the bodies of his victims in a graveyard and he always posed them lying on their backs with their arms across their chest. He also always left a single red rose lying across the victim's neck."

"And does that match what happened to Frannie?" Victoria asked.

"It does. To the letter."

"So why does this Deputy Colton think she may not have been a victim of the Strangler?"

"Little things, really. For one thing, the strangler was strong. The women he strangled died quickly, and it appeared he came up on them from behind because none of them had any defensive wounds. Frannie, however, appeared to have fought back. She had a bump on her head and defensive wounds on her hands and arms. While the autopsy didn't detail any discrepancies between Frannie and the other women, it was Ned's opinion she died much more slowly than the others, which could indicate the person who strangled her wasn't as strong or as skilled as the real Strangler."

"Did Deputy Colton consider the idea that Frannie was stronger than the other victims and therefore better able to fight back? That could have led the Strangler to be less effective in his attack." Jackson Jones—Jack for short—a dark-haired, blue-eyed, never-married nationally acclaimed author of hard-core mysteries and thrillers and my current love interest, asked.

"Yes, he did," I answered. "That was what the FBI believed. The difference in the killings could even be explained by something as simple as the Strangler being under the weather and therefore off his game. Ned told me that based on the data provided in the report it seemed as if Frannie may even have been knocked out and then strangled."

"So she fought back, either fell and hit her head, or her killer hit her in the head, causing her to pass out before being strangled," George Baxter, a writer of traditional whodunit mysteries, summarized. "That seems like a pretty big discrepancy to me."

"Ned and I agree. We both feel this case should have been given more attention than it was by the individuals investigating the Strangler."

"What else did the deputy have?" Jack asked.

"Ned also told me the roses the Strangler left were a long-stemmed, thornless variety. The rose left with

Frannie's body was long stemmed and red like the others but not thornless."

"Maybe he couldn't find a thornless rose when he killed Frannie," Brit speculated.

"No," Clara Kline, a self-proclaimed psychic who writes fantasy and paranormal mysteries, countered. "Serial killers are very methodical. They have a ritual that's very important to them that must be adhered to exactly if they're to obtain the emotional satisfaction or psychological relief normally brought to them by the kill. A serial killer wouldn't simply make a substitution. I think that's is an important clue."

"I agree with Clara, but it seems the FBI should have come to the same conclusion," Jack stated. "Why didn't they suspect a copycat?"

"Because of the tattoo," I said. "The Strangler carved a pentagram on the back of the right shoulder of every woman. The FBI kept that piece of information out of the press, so no one other than law enforcement knew about it. Frannie had the mark on her shoulder, the same as every other woman. What I'm asking you to do is help me determine whether Frannie K. was the fourth victim of the Silk Stocking Strangler or if she was killed by someone else who used the hype created by the serial killer to try to get away with murder. I know the anomalies are small, but according to Deputy Colton, the FBI determined Frannie was a victim of the Strangler and never considered any other suspects."

"Do *we* have other suspects?" George asked.

"Not really," I admitted. "At least not yet."

"Were you ever able to identify the man who wrote the letters?" George asked.

"I've been unable to definitively identify him, but Deputy Savage managed to obtain the original FBI report. While the Paul in the letters never gave his last name, the FBI determined Frannie's husband Tom had a brother named Paul. While we don't know this for certain, we're assuming the writer of the letters was Frannie's brother-in-law. We haven't been able to track down Paul Kettleman to verify it."

"And Tom?" George asked.

"We've been able to confirm that in August 1964 Tom was sent back to the States after suffering a head injury. Five days after he arrived in South Carolina, Frannie was dead. Tom died eleven months after Frannie was murdered as a result of complications from the head injury he received in Vietnam."

"So if the Strangler didn't kill Frannie her husband must have done it," Brit surmised.

"Maybe. Based on the letters Paul sent, he was concerned for Frannie's safety when Tom came home, although it may be hard to prove he killed her. We certainly won't be able to get a confession from him. Still, we do have something to work with. Ned has expressed an interest in working with us should we decide to pursue the case. He has the file he created at the time of the murder, which he feels should be reexamined. Additionally, I've gathered the names of several people who still live on the island who knew Frannie when she lived here. I thought we'd speak to them. If we can get a better idea of exactly what was going on in Frannie's life at the time she was killed, other suspects may begin to emerge. Jack and I have already decided to take a stab at figuring this out. Is anyone else in?"

The room fell quiet. I decided to give everyone a minute to process what I'd shared with them. It was a lot to take in and a lot of years had passed. This wasn't going to be an easy case to tackle.

"Mystery solved, Mystery solved," Blackbeard, my brother Garrett's parrot, broke the silence.

I laughed. "It looks like Blackbeard's in." I looked at the large bird. "I guess I should have asked you if you had anything to add." Blackbeard had been instrumental in solving mysteries in the past, although he most definitely hadn't been living at the resort when Frannie did. I doubted he was even alive, but parrots could live eighty or more years and I had no idea how old he was, so I supposed it was possible. Garrett had told me that he'd found Blackbeard, or more accurately, Blackbeard had found him. Garrett had been near the beach when Blackbeard flew up and landed on his shoulder. They'd been friends ever since.

"The solution to this mystery isn't going to be that easy," Brit joined in. "You all know I'm involved in the local production of *A Christmas Carol*, which runs from December 20 to December 22. We have an aggressive rehearsal schedule until then, so I'm not sure to what extent I can help, but I'm happy to help if I can. My specialty is really social media and I don't think that will come into play in a fifty-year-old case, but if you need me to research anything, just holler."

"Thanks," I responded. "I appreciate that."

Alex spoke next. "As you know, I'm pretty busy trying to finish my book on Trey Alderman, but if you need something specific, just ask."

"I have some time," George said. "I'm digging into my books, but I can do some research on the strangler. It does seem like an interesting case."

"Great; thanks." I smiled.

"You know I'm in," Vikki said, jumped onto the bandwagon. "I've been captivated by Frannie's story since you first showed me the letters. I think we can depend on help from Rick as well." Vikki was referring to Deputy Rick Savage, the acting deputy in charge on the island and Vikki's current love interest. "We've discussed the matter a few times and I can tell he's intrigued."

"And I as well," Clara voiced. "You can't help but wonder what really happened to that poor woman. I've been meditating on the necklace you found with the letters and I think I'm close to establishing an emotional link with her spirit."

"Okay. Let's decide on a date so whoever's available can get back together. Jack and I have interviews set up for the next two days and then we're working at the tree lot on Wednesday afternoon. How about Thursday or Friday?"

"Friday evening works best for me because we don't have rehearsal then," Brit said.

"I can do Friday," Vikki seconded.

Everyone else agreed, so we set Friday evening as six for our next meeting. I volunteered to make dinner. George requested lasagna and Clara wanted garlic bread, so it seemed we had our menu.

"I think that went well," Jack said as Clara headed upstairs and everyone else left for their cabins.

"I feel really drawn to this case. It's just so tragic. Whether Frannie was murdered by a serial killer or someone she knew and possibly loved, she was still just twenty years old. Twenty is much, much too young to have your life stolen from you."

Jack put his arm around my shoulders and pulled me close. "We've got a solid starting place and, I feel, a very good chance of finding out what really happened to Frannie."

"You sound optimistic."

"You know me: Jack Optimistic Jackson."

I smiled. "I do rather love that about you. So, where should we start?"

Jack removed his arm from around me and took a sheet of paper from his pocket. "Here are the interviews for the next two days. I'm between novels, but I do have a paper to run, so I thought I'd work in the morning and we could sleuth in the afternoons. We won't have a lot of time on Wednesday; we're supposed to be at the tree farm at four."

"What do we have tomorrow?"

"I know you spoke to Ned Colton on the phone, but I thought we should get a look at his file and maybe pick his brain a bit. I made an appointment to meet him at his home at one o'clock. I can pick you up at noon and we could grab a quick lunch first."

"That sounds good. Anyone else tomorrow?"

"Edna Turner. As you know, she was the town librarian at the time Frannie was murdered. When we spoke on the phone she told me that Frannie was an avid reader who came in to the library often. Edna expressed what seemed to be genuine grief over Frannie's death and indicated she was willing to help however she could. She seems to know a lot of people and I'm hoping she'll give us some additional leads. We're meeting with her at three o'clock. I thought we could go back to my place after that. I seem to remember you mentioning a willingness to help me decorate the place for the holiday."

"Sounds like fun. I think I may start decorating the resort tomorrow morning as well. As for tomorrow night, let's do pizza. I've been craving a good pizza for days."

"It's a date." Jack leaned over and gave me a quick kiss on the lips.

"And what does Wednesday look like?"

"I've made two appointments for the early afternoon. We're seeing Sherry Pierce, who was a friend of Frannie when she lived on the island at noon, and Roland Carver, who was the mayor at the time of the murder, at two o'clock. After that we'll need to head to the tree lot for our shift."

"I can't wait to get started."

After Jack left I grabbed a sweater and went out onto the patio. It was a clear night and the stars in the sky looked like diamonds on a bed of black velvet. The nights had grown cooler as the days had grown shorter, but I still enjoyed spending a few minutes looking out over the vastness of the ocean before I went to bed.

I loved the fact that I could hear the sound of the sea from my bedroom in the attic. It was calming to let the natural rhythm of the waves lull me to sleep. When I'd first moved to Gull Island from New York, I'd missed the sound of traffic, but now that I'd been on the island for six months the hustle and bustle of the city didn't possess the same appeal it once had.

"I see you had the same idea I did," Vikki said as I walked slowly along the white sand beach.

"It's a lovely evening," I agreed. "I'll admit the warmer climate doesn't quite mesh with the idea of Christmas, however."

"We should decorate the resort. We can string white lights on the patio and around the eaves of the cabins. The main house will be a bit more challenging, but I'm sure we can get the guys to help."

"I've been thinking about decorating. I'd love to do a tree in the living room of the main house. There are some boxes of decorations in the spare room. I'll take a look tomorrow to see what we have. Will you be here for Christmas?"

"I'm planning to spend Christmas Eve and Christmas Day with Rick. We're invited to his brother's for Christmas dinner."

"We should have a big dinner here at the resort earlier in the week. Maybe the twenty-third?"

"Alex is going to the Bahamas on the twenty-third. How about the twenty-second? Brit's play is wrapping up that night, but it's an early performance, so she should be done by seven. We can have a late dinner afterward."

"I love the idea. I'll check with the others." I looked out toward the calm sea. "I think I'll head in. I'll see you in the morning."

"I'm heading out early to meet with my agent. I'll stop and stock up on twinkle lights while I'm in Charleston. Maybe we can start decorating tomorrow evening. I can't wait to turn this place into a Christmas fairyland."

I went back into the house, locked up, and headed up to my room. I grabbed some pajamas from my dresser and went into my attached bathroom. I changed and washed up, then went back into the bedroom. I was tired and it was late, but for some reason I was oddly antsy. Deciding to watch TV for a few minutes, I dug around in my nightstand for the remote. A piece of paper fell to the floor as I pulled out the remote from the drawer. Leaning over, I picked it up and was about to toss it back in the drawer when I noticed the message, penned with pink ink. It was a reminder I'd made to myself to follow up on a lead I'd been provided regarding a freelance article I planned to write detailing the secret behind a real-life local Santa. Local restaurant owner Gertie Newsome had told me about the local legend a week ago and it had immediately piqued my interest.

It seemed that twelve years ago a fire on the north end of the island had destroyed four homes. Three of them were vacation homes, but the fourth was a primary residence, and the family who lived there had lost everything. The fire had occurred just a week before Christmas, making the pain of loss all that much more acute. The family didn't have insurance that paid for a temporary rental and it looked as if they might actually be homeless until an anonymous donor paid for a furnished rental nearby. When the family arrived at their temporary home, not only was the home fully stocked with food, clothing, and other items they'd need, but there was a large decorated tree in the living room with dozens of colorfully wrapped gifts placed beneath.

The person who'd saved Christmas for this family was never identified and it was assumed the benefactor's generosity was a onetime thing. The story was mainly forgotten until the next year, when the local animal shelter was about to be shut down due to the loss of their facility, until Secret Santa, as everyone began calling him, anonymously donated an alternate building which was still being used to this day.

Every year since, a person, family, business, or animal in need had been gifted with their own Christmas miracle. Jack had written a nice article for the local paper, but if I wanted to interest a national publication in the story, I'd need to dig deeper to identify the person behind the legend. My mind played with idea as to how exactly I would accomplish this as I drifted off to sleep with a smile on my face.

Recipes from Readers

Scones with a Flavor Twist—submitted by Joanne Kocourek
Nana's Banana Bread—submitted by Darla Taylor
No-Name Cake—submitted by Patty Liu
Tropical Treat Bread—submitted by Vivian Shane

Scones with a Flavor Twist

Submitted by Joanne Kocourek

These are wonderful! Best I've had in a long time. I've tried baking scones before and never liked the outcome. I tweaked the recipe a bit, though, because I wanted to offer a variety of flavors.

Base Ingredients:
2 cups all-purpose flour
⅓ cup sugar
1 tbs. baking powder
½ tsp. salt
½ cup cold butter, cut into ½-inch cubes
1 cup whipping cream, divided
Wax paper

Sweet Variation Ingredients:
Chocolate-cherry scones: Stir in ¼ cup dried cherries, coarsely chopped, and 2 oz. coarsely chopped semisweet chocolate with the cream.
Apricot-ginger scones: Stir in ½ cup finely chopped dried apricots and 2 tbs. finely chopped crystallized ginger with the cream. Drizzle with vanilla glaze after baking.
Cranberry-pistachio scones: Stir in ¼ cup sweetened dried cranberries and ¼ cup coarsely chopped roasted salted pistachios with the cream.

Brown sugar-pecan scones: Substitute brown sugar for granulated sugar. Stir in ½ cup chopped toasted pecans with the cream.

Glaze Ingredients:
1 cup confectioners' sugar
3 tbs. heavy cream (or half-and-half or milk)
¼ tsp. vanilla extract

To make the glaze, simply whisk all the glaze ingredients together and drizzle lightly over scones right before serving. Scones are best enjoyed fresh from the oven.

Preheat oven to 450 degrees. Stir together first four ingredients in a large bowl. Cut butter into flour mixture with a pastry blender until crumbly and mixture resembles small peas. Freeze 5 minutes. Add ¾ cup plus 2 tbs. cream, stirring until dry ingredients are just moistened.

Turn dough out onto wax paper; gently press or pat dough into a 7-inch round (mixture will be crumbly). Cut round into 8 wedges. Place wedges 2 inches apart on a lightly greased baking sheet. Brush tops of wedges with remaining 2 tbs. cream until just moistened.

Bake at 375 degrees for 15–20 minutes or until tops are golden brown.

Nana's Banana Bread

Submitted by Darla Taylor

1 cup sugar
½ cup butter (1 stick)
1 egg, beaten
3–5 overripe bananas, mashed
2 cups flour
1 tsp. baking soda
1 cup nuts (walnuts or pecans, optional)

Preheat oven to 350 degrees. Grease a loaf pan (may need two).

Mixing by hand, blend sugar and butter until creamy. Add the rest of the ingredients. Mix well. Spread mixture into pan(s).

Bake approximately 1 hour until toothpick inserted in center comes out clean.

No-Name Cake

Submitted by Patty Liu

1 pkg. yellow cake mix
1 large can pineapple, crushed
1 cup sugar
1 pkg. (6-serving size) Jell-O Instant Vanilla Pudding
Mix; prepare according to package directions
1 large container Cool Whip, thawed
Flaked coconut (toasted, if desired)

Prepare according to directions and bake cake in a 9 x
13 x 2–inch pan according to directions. Bring
pineapple and sugar to a boil, then let cool
completely. Once baked cake has cooled, poke holes
in it with a fork and pour pineapple mixture over it;
drain excess juice prior to pouring over cake. Spread
prepared pudding over top of pineapple layer;
refrigerate. Shortly before serving, spread Cool Whip
over cake and sprinkle with coconut, if desired.

Serves 12–14

Tropical Treat Bread

Submitted by Vivian Shane

This yummy bread tastes like carrot cake but with a coconut twist! I always try to fool myself that I'm only making this as a way to get more fruit and veggies into my diet….

3 cups flour
2 cups sugar
1 tsp. baking soda
1 tsp. cinnamon
¾ tsp. salt
3 eggs
1½ cups carrots
¼ cup flaked coconut
¼ cup golden raisins
8-oz. can unsweetened crushed pineapple, drained
1 cup vegetable oil (I've substituted applesauce for the oil)
1 cup pecans
2 tsp. vanilla

In a large bowl, combine flour, sugar, baking soda, cinnamon, and salt. In another bowl, beat the eggs. Add carrots, coconut, raisins, pineapple, vegetable oil, pecans, and vanilla and stir to combine. Stir this mixture into the dry ingredients until just moistened.

Spoon into two greased and floured 4 x 8 x 2–loaf
pans. Bake at 350 degrees for 65–75 minutes or until
a toothpick inserted in center comes out clean. Cool
in pan for 15 minutes, then remove and cool
completely on wire rack.

I occasionally drizzle the top with some ready-made
cream cheese frosting thinned down with milk to
make it drizzle consistency.

Books by Kathi Daley

Come for the murder, stay for the romance.

Zoe Donovan Cozy Mystery:
Halloween Hijinks
The Trouble With Turkeys
Christmas Crazy
Cupid's Curse
Big Bunny Bump-off
Beach Blanket Barbie
Maui Madness
Derby Divas
Haunted Hamlet
Turkeys, Tuxes, and Tabbies
Christmas Cozy
Alaskan Alliance
Matrimony Meltdown
Soul Surrender
Heavenly Honeymoon
Hopscotch Homicide
Ghostly Graveyard
Santa Sleuth
Shamrock Shenanigans
Kitten Kaboodle
Costume Catastrophe
Candy Cane Caper
Holiday Hangover
Easter Escapade
Camp Carter
Trick or Treason
Reindeer Roundup – *December 2017*

Zimmerman Academy The New Normal

Tj Jensen Paradise Lake Mysteries by Henery Press:

Pumpkins in Paradise
Snowmen in Paradise
Bikinis in Paradise
Christmas in Paradise
Puppies in Paradise
Halloween in Paradise
Treasure in Paradise
Fireworks in Paradise – *October 2017*
Beaches in Paradise – *June 2018*

Whales and Tails Cozy Mystery:

Romeow and Juliet
The Mad Catter
Grimm's Furry Tail
Much Ado About Felines
Legend of Tabby Hollow
Cat of Christmas Past
A Tale of Two Tabbies
The Great Catsby
Count Catula
The Cat of Christmas Present
A Winter's Tail
The Taming of the Tabby
Frankencat
The Cat of Christmas Future – *November 2017*
The Cat of New Orleans – *February 2018*

Seacliff High Mystery:

The Secret
The Curse
The Relic
The Conspiracy
The Grudge
The Shadow
The Haunting

Sand and Sea Hawaiian Mystery:
Murder at Dolphin Bay
Murder at Sunrise Beach
Murder at the Witching Hour
Murder at Christmas
Murder at Turtle Cove
Murder at Water's Edge
Murder at Midnight

Writers' Retreat Southern Mystery:
First Case
Second Look
Third Strike
Fourth Victim – *October 2017*
Fifth Night – *January 2018*

Rescue Alaska Paranormal Mystery:
Finding Justice – *November 2017*

A Tess and Tilly Mystery:
The Christmas Letter – *December 2017*

Road to Christmas Romance:
Road to Christmas Past
    USA Today bestselling author, Kathi Daley, lives in beautiful Lake Tahoe with her husband Ken. When

she isn't writing, she likes spend time hiking the miles of desolate trails surrounding her home. She has authored more than seventy five books in eight series including: Zoe Donovan Cozy Mysteries, Whales and Tails Island Mysteries, Sand and Sea Hawaiian Mysteries, Tj Jensen Paradise Lake Series, Writer's Retreat Southern Seashore Mysteries, Rescue Alaska Paranormal Mysteries, Tess and Tilly Cozy Mystery Series, and Seacliff High Teen Mysteries. Find out more about her books at **www.kathidaley.com**

Giveaway:

I do a giveaway for books, swag, and gift cards every week in my newsletter, *The Daley Weekly* **http://eepurl.com/NRPDf**

Other links to check out:
Kathi Daley Blog – publishes each Friday
http://kathidaleyblog.com
Facebook at Kathi Daley Books –
www.facebook.com/kathidaleybooks
Kathi Daley Books Group Page –
https://www.facebook.com/groups/569578823146850/
E-mail – **kathidaley@kathidaley.com**
Twitter at Kathi Daley@kathidaley –
https://twitter.com/kathidaley
Amazon Author Page –
https://www.amazon.com/author/kathidaley
BookBub – **https://www.bookbub.com/authors/kathi-daley**

89617622R10102

Made in the USA
Middletown, DE
17 September 2018